Spotted Leaves

Also by Zenda Vecchio and published by Ginninderra Press

Mavis

A Conversation with Emily

Children at the Gate

Tiger! Tiger!

Light on Dark Water

Becoming Kirsty-Lee

The Swan's Egg

Fractals (Pocket Poets)

Spindrift

Zenda Vecchio

Spotted Leaves

Selected Stories

Spotted Leaves: Selected Stories
ISBN 978 1 74027 957 4
Copyright © text Zenda Vecchio 2015
Cover photo © Ginninderra Press 2015

This collection first published 2015 by
Ginninderra Press
PO Box 3461 Port Adelaide 5015
www.ginninderrapress.com.au

Contents

from *A Conversation with Emily and other stories* — 7

A Conversation with Emily — 9

A Smile from Leah — 12

Talking to Sophie — 19

Because of Rose — 26

Losing Laura — 30

from *Children at the Gate* — **41**

Dark Gods of the Woods — 43

Lisa Had Brown Eyes — 48

An Egret Flying — 60

Hounds of the Hunter — 67

Marigold Flower — 69

Blood on the Snow — 72

from *Tiger! Tiger!* — **77**

Tiger — 79

Burning Bright — 99

In the Forests of the Night — 113

The Lamb — 119

from *Light on Dark Water* — **123**

Butterflies — 125

Hair Ribbons — 128

Baby Crying   135

Blue Plate   140

Angus   144

The Plum Tree   151

Girl with Fair Hair   155

Dilly   159

Moth   165

The Lady of Shalott   170

from *A Conversation with Emily
and other stories*

A Conversation with Emily

Yesterday afternoon I found Emily in the corner of my mind.

She was sitting on a stool by the window, watching the rain. There was something old-fashioned about her. Perhaps it was her dress. It was navy blue and high-waisted and looked too big for her. Or maybe it was the way her hair, tied with red ribbon, tumbled down her back, curling at the ends. It was the kind of brown you knew would shine gold in the sun.

When she heard me approach, she turned. 'Oh, it's you,' she said with a marked lack of enthusiasm.

I felt a little affronted. 'Who did you expect?' I asked, but she just shrugged and went back to staring out of the window.

'Did you think perhaps I was your mother coming to fetch you?'

Emily sighed. She shifted her stool so she sat facing me, but she did not look at me. Instead, she played with the folds of her dress. I saw now that it was beautifully hand-smocked across the bodice. Her hair fell forward, shielding her. I longed to brush it aside but I knew she did not want me to touch her. 'I haven't met your parents yet,' I said.

'I know.' Then she brightened. 'I was wondering. Do you think I could have a brother? Just an ordinary one. I've planned him all out. He's about twelve, with freckles and a thatch of brown hair that hangs over his eyes. Barney, that's his name. He's got one of those little black and white dogs, a fox terrier I think, called Toby and...' She paused for breath.

'Oh, Emily,' I said helplessly, knowing already I could not refuse her. 'What sort of name is Barney? I'm sure children aren't called that now.'

She set her mouth stubbornly. 'I can't help that,' she said. 'It's his name. Oh, he's going to be such fun. He's in the shed now making a bow and arrow. He's even going to make a little one for me. As soon as it stops raining, we're going to hunt the magpie.'

'Hunt the magpie?' I repeated, wondering if I had heard her properly.

It sounded so odd. Hunt the dragon, the dinosaur, even the wild boar. But the magpie…?

'Yes,' Emily explained seriously. 'There's a pair of magpies nesting in the gum trees by the gate. They keep swooping on us. Yesterday they nearly got my little sister Alicia.'

'You've got a sister too?' I asked, a little put out. After all, this was my province.

Emily looked uncomfortable. 'Well, I'd like one. A baby one that has just started to walk. Oh, she's so sweet with dimples and curls and…'

'I think you're forgetting a few things,' I interrupted. 'I am the writer. I am the one who decides.'

'I know, I know.' Emily leaned forward, her face flushed and earnest. 'I don't mean to offend you. Truly. It's just what I'd like. Of course,' she shrugged, pretending indifference, 'you can change them. I hope you don't, though.' Her voice faltered. 'We're all in your power, I know that. I don't blame you. I understand.' She sighed and looked away. 'That's the trouble with a story. It can't be about happy people. You've got to have tension and drama and…and conflict.' She looked down at her hands. 'I hate conflict,' she whispered. 'All that shouting. I'm so afraid of what you're going to do to Mummy and Daddy. I know you have to do something. I mean, look at me – my dress, my Italian leather boots. It's obvious we're well off, and that makes it worse. Because, if we were poor, that might be enough, us against our environment, us just surviving. But since we're rich, it means the conflict has to be in us, in them. Oh!' she cried passionately. 'What are you going to do to my mummy and daddy?'

I felt stricken. I wanted to explain it wasn't my fault. It was the creative process. We were both at its mercy. But I didn't know how to tell her that.

'Even my name,' Emily continued sadly. 'Yesterday, before I came, I heard you say you thought Emily a plaintive sort of name. And it is. Oh, why couldn't you have called me Felicity – that means happiness. I saw it in your name book and I hoped and hoped that's what you'd call me.'

'Oh, Emily.' I shook my head. 'Felicity looks quite different from you.'

Suddenly I couldn't help myself. I reached out and put my arms around her. Emily clung to me sobbing.

It was then I made up my mind. I wiped her face with my handkerchief and pulled her on to my lap. 'Listen, Emily, it's quite true, what you say. I mean you wouldn't have much of a story if everyone in it was happy all the time.'

'If people like being happy, why don't they like reading about it?' Emily whispered, her face hidden against me.

'Well, they do. They like happy endings. Or at least they used to. I'm not sure what they like now. Some modern stories don't even make sense.' I laughed a little bitterly, because of course those stories are the most successful and I haven't yet learned how to write one.

'You know, Emily, I've been thinking, we don't have to put you in a story at all.'

Emily sat bolt upright and stared at me. 'But wouldn't that mean I wouldn't exist? I'd be just nothing.'

'Of course not. You're here now, aren't you? No, what I mean is we'll invent you a whole wonderful life, a nice mummy and daddy, and you'll have Barney and Alicia too of course. Now what else – oh, a big old house and, I know, an orchard. You must have an orchard, Emily, so you can play there in spring. Imagine the blossom falling like confetti. Yes, and we'll have daffodils growing there and...'

'A pony,' whispered Emily. 'Could I have a little, black, shaggy pony?'

'Of course, and a cat with kittens in the barn. And a wild, overgrown garden. Wet lilac – oh, Emily, the scent of lilacs in the evening after rain.'

Emily's eyes were shining like stars.

I caught my breath. For some reason, I felt close to tears. 'When we've finished everything,' I told her gently, 'we'll leave it be, all complete. I promise you I won't ever put you in a story. You'll be safe with your family. Only sometimes, when I'm lonely, I'll come and see how you're getting on.'

Emily put her arms around my neck and held her soft little cheek against mine. 'Do you think,' she whispered, 'do you think my mummy could be kind of like you?'

A Smile from Leah

It was raining when Kate came out of the doctor's surgery. She stared at the sullen sky, surprised. Only a few hours before, when she had taken Leah to Sally Spencer's birthday party, it had been bright and sunny. But autumn was like that. Capricious. She could never understand why people found it beautiful. The brilliant leaves, the clarity of light, the opulence of ripening fruit, all of it was a mask to hide the coming of winter.

Kate shivered and pulled up the collar of her thin jacket. She hoped Leah wasn't cold. Foolish of her not to have insisted the little girl take her cardigan. But her dress was so pretty, pale green broderie anglaise with a wide ribbon sash and little puff sleeves. Leah herself had chosen the pattern and even helped her mother make it on the machine. Such a darling, old-fashioned little girl. She was so lucky. After two boys, the daughter she had always dreamed of. And Leah was so pretty, with her blue eyes and red-gold curls. Ah, that was autumn for you if you liked – Leah's hair cascading down her back; Leah dancing, laughing, red-cheeked like a scarlet leaf caught in the wind.

A sudden squall of rain blew into her face. Kate stepped from the shelter of the doorway and hurried across the road to her car. No time for dreaming. She'd be late picking up Leah. And it was silly to worry about Leah being cold; the children'd be inside on a day like this, playing games. She had a sudden vivid picture of a group of little girls, bright as butterflies in their party dresses, playing pass-the-parcel.

She swung the car onto the main road and headed out into the country. The Spencers lived a mile or so out of town. They were well-off, the kind of people who wanted to give their children every advantage, a nice house, a few acres of land, even a pony for Sally. Next thing, Leah would be begging for a pony too. Oh well, she'd just have to talk John round. They could probably afford it…

Now, was this the turn-off. It was difficult to tell. It was getting dark already. Confusing, the bare paddocks, the clumps of trees – all these places looked disconcertingly alike in the half-light. She'd never actually met the Spencers, but Leah had had no trouble directing her. 'That's it,' she'd announced, bouncing up and down on the seat. 'See the balloons on the gate.' Kate had been running late for her doctor's appointment so she'd just dropped her off with a quick kiss. No need to remind Leah to use her manners. Not like the boys. Kate grinned ruefully. Kane and Ethan were quite a different story.

Ah, this was the right house. She remembered the willow tree at the front. Strange that, in the afternoon sunshine, the willow had looked welcoming, its trailing branches green, tipped with gold. But now it was somehow menacing. She gave an involuntary shudder. She put her foot on the brake and the car jerked to a stop.

She sat in the car for a moment trying to control her emotions. For some reason she didn't want to walk past the willow tree. It writhed in the wind like a live thing.

'This is ridiculous,' she told herself sternly, fumbling in her handbag for a packet of cigarettes. Leah didn't like her smoking. Such a caring little girl. 'Please, Mummy,' she had begged, tears running down her cheeks. 'See, it's right here on the packet, Smoking is dangerous for your health.' In the end, Kate pretended she had given up. She couldn't bear to see Leah upset.

Calm at last, Kate unlocked the car door and stepped bravely out, averting her eyes as she passed the willow tree. The front door opened at her first knock. A woman of about her own age stood there, her soft brown hair streaked with grey, her eyes, kind, questioning, framed by a pair of thick glasses. She was dressed unfashionably in an old beige skirt and cardigan yet there was something about her – grace, dignity, self-assurance – that gave her an aura almost of elegance.

'I'm sorry I'm late,' Kate said. 'I've come for Leah.'

'Leah?' repeated the woman, raising one delicate eyebrow. 'I'm afraid I don't understand.'

Kate blinked. Her mouth went dry. Surely she hadn't come to the wrong house after all. 'Mrs Spencer?' she said and, when the other woman nodded, Kate hurried on, 'I've come for my daughter, Leah Thomas. I left her here earlier for a birthday party.'

The woman frowned. Her brown eyes were concerned. 'Perhaps you'd better come in,' she suggested. 'There must be some mistake. Sally did have a party this afternoon. But there wasn't any little girl called Leah here. I'm sure of it.'

'But…but…Leah had an invitation. This address. She even had a map. Sally drew her a map…' Kate's voice trailed away.

The other woman held the door open and Kate stumbled in after her. Once in the sitting room she sank down, uninvited, in one of the easy chairs. She looked around her, dazed. It was a casual, friendly room, a vase of cosmos and Queen Anne's lace on a corner table, an old-fashioned dresser with a display of gleaming plates, a boy's denim jacket flung carelessly on the settee. A lank, black cat stretched itself insolently by the fire.

'Please,' whispered Kate, 'Leah must be here. I brought her to this house this afternoon. We had a present for Sally's birthday – a book about horses, *Black Beauty*, because Leah said Sally had a pony and…' She shook her head. She stared down at her hands. They were clasping and unclasping themselves in her lap. 'I was late for my doctor's appointment. Otherwise I would have brought her to the front door and introduced myself. I… There were balloons on the gate, pink and yellow ones tied with a gold ribbon. Leah said how pretty they were…' Her head jerked up and she stared desperately at Sally's mother. 'If she's not here, where is she? What have you done with my Leah? You…' She lurched to her feet. 'Leah. Leah,' she shouted. 'Mummy's here. Where are you? Leah…'

The other woman crossed quickly to her side. She tried to put a reassuring arm around Kate. 'It's all right, dear. We'll find her. I promise, we'll find her. Now, you just sit down for a moment. That's right. I'll get you a glass of water and then we'll work out what to do.' She paused on her way to the door. 'I'll just call the children. Maybe they can help us.'

She returned a few moments later with a girl and boy. The girl, Sally, was nowhere near as pretty as Leah but she had an open, friendly little face, a scattering of freckles across a pert nose, brown hair in two short pigtails. The boy, taller, was dark-haired and serious. He had his mother's air of quiet dignity. Kate warmed to him at once.

As soon as he saw her, he gave her a wide smile. 'Hello, Mrs Thomas,' he said. 'Mum didn't tell us it was you.'

'You…you know me?' stammered Kate, putting out a hand and laying it on his arm. There was something dependable about him. He could be trusted. She was by no means so sure of his mother and sister.

''Course. You're Kane's mother. I met you last year at sports day. You congratulated me when I won the under-twelve trophy.'

Kate nodded. She said eagerly, 'Then…then, if you know Kane, you must know Leah, his little sister. She's nine like Sally. They're in grade four together.'

The boy looked puzzled. He glanced at his sister. 'I don't think… Sally, do you know Leah? I know Ethan, of course, your other boy. We play football together but…'

'There isn't any Leah in my class,' interrupted the little girl, brightly. 'I don't think there's anyone called Leah in the whole school.'

All at once, Kate wanted to slap her. She had difficulty holding her hands still. Only the boy's steady eyes helped her. I'm glad she's not really Leah's friend, Kate decided. Brash little thing. So sure of herself. And she's lying.

Suddenly she reached out and grabbed the little girl's arm, pulling her closer. 'You listen to me, miss,' she said through clenched teeth. 'Leah had an invitation. I saw it. And a map drawn by you. If you don't know Leah, why did you invite her to your party?'

Sally was frightened. Kate was glad. Nasty little thing. She glared at her. Sally wrenched herself free and ran to her mother. She began to whimper. Mrs Spencer bent down and embraced her.

'I wrote out the invitations,' she said quietly. Her voice was no longer friendly.

Kate turned away and stared into the fire. She didn't want to hear what the other woman was saying but Mrs Spencer went on relentlessly.

'We invited five little girls, all known to me, all in Sally's class. We didn't invite anyone called Leah. And she never came. If you dropped her off as you say, then she never knocked at the front door, never made herself known to us. Unless…' she turned to her son. 'You were outside all afternoon, Morris. Did you see a little girl?'

The boy shook his head. He was frowning. But he wasn't hostile. Not like Mrs Spencer and Sally. He had nothing to hide.

'I want you to call the police,' shouted Kate hysterically. 'Now! Immediately! There's something going on here and I don't like it!'

When Mrs Spencer seemed to hesitate, Kate shouted even louder. 'Yes, the police. They'll make you tell them what you've done with my baby.'

'Wait a minute.' The boy, Morris, interrupted. He sat down next to Kate. 'Have you got a photo of Leah with you? Maybe if Sally and I knew what she looked like, we'd know if we'd ever seen her.'

Kate smiled at him gratefully. 'Yes, yes, of course.' She opened her handbag and scrabbled through its contents. At last she produced a dog-eared photograph. She held it out triumphantly. Then, all at once, her expression changed. She stared at the photo, frowning. 'But it can't be… Look, Morris…Leah isn't there. She…' She raised dark, tormented eyes to the boy's face. 'How could that happen?' she whispered. 'How could a little girl disappear from a photograph? See, John's there and the boys, Kane and Ethan…' She staggered to her feet and took a step or two towards Mrs Spencer and Sally. 'How did you do that? How did you make Leah disappear from my photo? I…' She put her hands over her face and sank down again, sobbing.

In a moment, Mrs Spencer was at her side. She put her arms around her. 'It's all right, my dear. Don't upset yourself any more. What I think we should do, is telephone your husband. John, did you say his name was? You've got yourself confused. Yes, that's it. You know, I wouldn't be surprised if Leah has been home with him all this time. Let me call him and he'll come and get you. You can't drive home like this. Leah isn't here. I'm sure she's home with her father and brothers.'

Kate clung to her like a child to its mother. 'Do you think so? Oh, do you really think so? Yes, yes, you'd better ring John. The number… the number's in my wallet…' She tried to smile. 'I'm always forgetting my telephone number. John made me write it down on a card and put it in my wallet.'

Mrs Spencer took her wallet and went into the hallway. Kate could hear her voice as she talked to John. She sighed. She didn't really want him to come. He would be so cross. Still, there was nothing else she could do. Obviously, neither Mrs Spencer nor Sally was going to tell her where Leah was. It was always the same. People, ordinary, harmless-looking people made Leah disappear. But they wouldn't admit to it. Oh, they pretended to be so kind, made all sorts of useless suggestions, but the truth was, they didn't care. Mrs Spencer had her little girl, why should she care about Kate's?

John arrived half an hour later. Kate ignored him. She drank the sweet tea they gave her and swallowed her pills. She stared at the fire. There, in the heart of the flames, wasn't that Leah's sweet, flower-like face? Eagerly she reached out her hands but John grabbed her roughly and pushed her back into her chair. John was so cruel. He didn't want her to find Leah. He was jealous because she loved Leah so much. He'd probably helped Mrs Spencer make Leah disappear. He certainly seemed friendly enough with her. You couldn't trust John. Years ago, he'd let himself be convinced that Leah was dead, though she'd told him they were lying. How could anyone as beautiful as Leah be killed? A car accident, they said. As if she'd let anything like that happen to her little girl. She was such a careful driver. Anyway, the day of the accident, she'd left Leah playing in the garden at home. She must have, because Leah wasn't killed, wasn't even hurt…

In the end, though, she'd had to pretend to agree with them. Otherwise they'd have never let her out of the hospital. And Kane and Ethan and Leah needed her. You couldn't be a mother to your children if they kept you locked away. Or a wife either. Not that John deserved a wife. He'd betrayed her, her and Leah. He'd denied his own little girl. Still, she had to be careful. She had to cooperate or he might take her back to the hospital. He insisted she see the doctor every fortnight, that was bad enough…

Oh, if only John would convince Mrs Spencer to give Leah back. They could all be friends then, have tea together perhaps. She wouldn't hold it against them, how they'd tricked her… If only they'd tell her where Leah was… Sally could come over to play every day, Leah'd show her her room, her collection of dolls, they could pick flowers in Leah's own little garden…

Kate put her hands over her face. She began to cry quietly. Because it wasn't going to happen. Not ever. They weren't going to help her. John was telling the Spencers about her doctor. He wasn't even mentioning Leah. She'd have to find Leah all by herself. She was so tired. She hoped it wouldn't take long. They were right about one thing, though. Leah wasn't here any longer. But that didn't matter. Sooner or later she'd find her again. She always did.

Kate got to her feet. 'Take me home,' she demanded. She was careful not to look at Mrs Spencer or Sally. But her eyes lingered for a moment on the boy. Such a kind boy…and kindness was so rare. Because the boy believed her. He knew Leah was alive. She could see it in his face. She made a small gesture toward him. 'Thank you,' she said.

The boy gave her an uncertain smile.

She nodded to herself. Yes, he was special all right. Because that was Leah's smile. Exactly. That was how Leah smiled when she was unsure of herself. Shy. Full of sweetness.

With a suddenly light heart, Kate walked unsteadily to her husband's car. She carried Leah's smile with her like a shield. All the way home she held it carefully in her hands so John couldn't see it.

Talking to Sophie

As soon as the shouting began, Emma ran outside to the Hiding Place. Sophie was already there. Emma could see the pink of her dress through the overhanging branches. Carefully she tunnelled her way in. Sophie turned to smile but she did not speak. She was playing with some leaves and small stones.

Panting, Emma leaned against the corrugated iron fence and watched her. The dappled light and shade wavered with the wind. Sophie's lashes were dark against the curve of her cheek, her little hands, moving, made a pattern in the air just as intricate as the pattern of leaves and stones on the ground. Yes, thought Emma, momentarily distracted, Sophie's hands are like white butterflies dancing. Abruptly she said, 'It was really bad this time. Mummy was crying. I think Daddy hit her, because her mouth was bleeding and all the side of her face was bruised.'

Sophie did not answer. Nor did her expression change. But she carefully collected a pile of leaves and stones and pushed them towards Emma. Reassured, Emma began making a design of her own.

Sophie sat back on her heels, watching. Now and then she bent forward to reposition a pebble or add a twig or two. 'We ought to get some flowers,' she said at last. 'Those little blue ones would look good.'

'Forget-me-nots.' Emma frowned. 'But not yet. Later. When it's safe.'

Suddenly they heard the back door slam.

Emma crouched down and held her breath. Other noises… footsteps…the garage door…the car…

'It's Daddy,' whispered Emma. 'He's gone somewhere.' She straightened up, brushing dirt from her dress. 'Maybe I'll go inside for a while. I'm awfully hungry. I'll get us something to eat, then I'll come back.'

'Okay.' Sophie started to rearrange her leaves. 'Bring back some blue flowers.'

Emma crawled out of the Hiding Place. She ran across the overgrown lawn and into the kitchen. Her brothers were there making peanut butter sandwiches.

When he saw her, Nick, the elder, grabbed the last slice of bread. 'Bad luck, Em,' he said cheerfully, his mouth full. 'There's none left. Hurry up, Chris. They're waiting for us at the oval.'

'Can I come?' asked Emma.

'No way.'

'But…but…'

'Oh, Nick,' interrupted Chris. 'We ought to let her. Just this once.'

Nick glared at him. 'Get real, Chris. She's a girl and a baby. You can play with her if you like, but I'm not. What d'you think the others'd say if we dragged her along?' He picked up his soccer ball and went out the door.

Without even glancing at Emma, Chris ran after him.

Emma's eyes stung. It wasn't fair. It was always the same. They had each other, while she was always alone. Then she remembered that Sophie was waiting. She found an old wrinkled apple and went outside to pick some forget-me-nots.

***

Night-time was the worst.

To begin with, the dark was always friendly. Emma cuddled down in the blankets and pretended she was a rabbit in a burrow. Safe. Cosy. The burrow was in a bank under an oak tree. Emma wasn't exactly sure she'd ever seen any oak trees but they were often mentioned in the stories the teacher read aloud on Friday afternoons. They sounded such strong trees. If you were a rabbit in a burrow protected by an oak, nothing bad could happen to you. Emma scrunched up her toes and hugged herself.

But you could never tell. At any time, her father's shouting could jerk her awake and then the dark was no longer comforting but full of menace. Emma lay rigid, clenching her hands, longing for Sophie.

Sophie would never come inside no matter how often Emma pleaded with her. Emma had a vague feeling that once, long ago, it had been different. But now, whenever she tried to talk about it, Sophie shut her mouth obstinately and concentrated on her patterns. Emma was obstinate too. 'I want you to stay the night,' she persisted. 'Just once.'

Sophie stopped playing but she didn't say anything.

Emma started to cry. 'Don't you like Mummy and Daddy?' she asked. 'Is that why you won't come?'

Sophie turned, startled, her eyes wide. 'Of course I like them. I love them. But…but…' Her voice faltered and she began pleating her dress with little nervous hands. 'I can't come inside. Oh, Emma, I wish I could but I can't.'

'I'm so frightened at night,' whispered Emma. 'If you were there, cuddled up to me, it would be all right.'

'I know. I know.' Sophie grabbed one of Emma's hands and held it tightly. 'I wish I could, really, but I can't, I can't.'

For a while there was silence, a scary kind of silence in which Emma thought she could hear things that weren't there. Not birds or the distant traffic but voices…

Then Sophie said, 'You know it's because of me they fight.'

'But…they…I mean, they don't even know about you. I've never told them and…'

'They know about me all right,' said Sophie in a flat kind of voice that Emma didn't like. 'They've always known. They keep blaming one another. And it's all so stupid. It wasn't anyone's fault. It just happened. And now they're spoiling everything. I wish…I wish I had never been born. Then it would be all right. They wouldn't miss me. They'd be happy with you and Chris and Nick.'

Emma stared at Sophie. She didn't understand. She shivered. Then a sudden thought struck her. 'Do you know Nick and Chris too?'

'Yes.'

'But you don't play with them, do you? I thought it was only me that could see you. I thought you…'

Sophie sighed. 'Oh, Emma.' She shook her head. 'I don't want to talk about it any more. Did you bring those red berries?'

But Emma wasn't going to be distracted so easily. 'I still don't see why you can't come inside one night and…'

'I know,' interrupted Sophie, her face brightening, 'we'll look for a special stone, one of those white, glittery ones. It'll protect you. Like magic.'

'Can a stone do that?'

'Course, if we want it to. You can hide it under your pillow at night and it'll be like I'm with you.'

Emma still looked doubtful. But when Sophie, frowning, began scrabbling through their pile of stones, she helped her. Usually, Sophie made her feel better. But this time Emma sensed it was different. She had to comfort Sophie.

***

Emma lay face down in the Hiding Place, sobbing. She heard Sophie push her way through. She made an effort to stop crying but it was quite a while before she succeeded. 'Oh, Sophie, something dreadful's happened. Daddy's gone away. He's not going to live with us any more.' She choked. 'They're getting divorced.'

Sophie stared at her, suddenly pale, her eyes big and dark. Emma was glad she didn't say anything. She was tired of people talking. It didn't change anything.

The night before, her mother had been unexpectedly gentle. She had sat Emma on her knee and put an arm around her. Emma longed for the comfort of leaning against her mother but something made her wary. Her mother said a lot of things that didn't make sense. How Daddy's leaving didn't mean he didn't love Emma. Of course he did – they both did – but sometimes grown-up people who were married stopped loving one another. Then it was best if they lived apart. Emma was glad then she'd refused to cuddle up to her mother. Because her mother was lying. If Daddy could stop loving Mummy, then he could just as easily stop loving Emma and probably already had. Otherwise he wouldn't have gone away without even saying goodbye. He would have found a way of making things all right with Mummy so he could go on being their father.

Emma had pushed her mother away and gone into her room and shut the door. She didn't want to listen any more. When her mother came in later to say goodnight, Emma turned to the wall and refused to answer.

When it was dark, Nick and Chris crept in. Chris climbed under the blankets with her but Nick sat on the end of her bed, swinging his legs. 'We've got to stick together now,' he said, 'you and Chris and me, Em. We've got to look after Mum now Dad's gone.'

'P'raps he'll come back,' ventured Chris hopefully.

'I wouldn't count on it.' Nick turned towards Emma. 'And I don't know why you keep snivelling, Emma. You know how scared you get when they fight. Well, that's over. You won't have to go and hide any more.'

Emma wondered how Nick had known she was crying. She had been careful not to make any noise. She wiped her eyes with the back of her hand. 'I don't want him to be gone,' she whispered.

'I know.'

Suddenly Emma realised Nick was just as bewildered as she and Chris. But he was the eldest. He had to pretend he didn't care.

'Things have been bad a long time. Ever since the baby died. That's when they started fighting.'

Emma's heart started to beat very fast. 'What baby?' she asked.

'Oh, you wouldn't remember. You were only little. So was Chris. They had a baby and she died and after that everything changed. Before… before…oh, it was good…they used to take us places. Mum was always laughing and Dad…Dad was never cross. Even when we were naughty he…'

'I remember,' interrupted Chris eagerly. 'We went to see Peter Pan and Tinkerbell gave me some pixie dust and I dropped it.'

'Yeah, and you howled the place down. I had to give you mine to shut you up.' Nick sighed. 'Come on, Chris. We'd better go to bed.' He opened the door. Emma could see his silhouette because of the dim hall light. He turned to face her. 'Go to sleep, Em,' he said gently. 'Don't cry any more. It'll be all right. I'll look after you. I promise.'

Emma wanted to tell Sophie how she felt. It was so confusing. She felt so many things at once. Anger and grief and fear. And relief. Because Nick was right. There wouldn't be any more shouting…and she felt ashamed because she was glad. It was overwhelming.

'Oh, Sophie,' whispered Emma. 'What are we going to do?'

Sophie didn't answer. She leaned forward and brushed the hair out of Emma's eyes. At last she said, 'Look, Emma, look at the birds playing on the lawn.'

Holding hands, they watched the sparrows through the concealing screen of leaves.

***

'I have had such a good day.' Emma flung herself down in the Hiding Place.

Sophie looked up at her expectantly, half–smiling.

'To begin with, the Push–Ups are back.' Emma paused to catch her breath. 'Nick said it was the end of them last year when the council sprayed them. He said no baby trees could cope with being poisoned as well as being covered with asphalt.'

'I've never seen a Push–Up,' said Sophie wistfully.

'Oh, they're so cute. Nick says they're poplar suckers but Chris and I call them Push–Ups cos that's what they do – push their way up through the footpath. You wouldn't think they could, would you? And they're so pretty – all greeny gold. Chris and I spent so long looking at them, Nick left us to go to school by ourselves.'

'And then?'

'Oh, the best day. After recess we had to write in our journals and mine was best. I got a gold star and then, in the afternoon, we had painting. Here, look.' Emma pulled a crumbled piece of butcher's paper out of her pocket. 'See. It's you making one of your patterns in the Hiding Place.'

Sophie examined the painting carefully. 'Oh, Emma, it's beautiful. You've even put in the forget–me–nots.'

'Mmm. Of course, I didn't tell them it was you. The teacher thought it was me.' Emma considered the picture for a moment, her head on one side. 'You know, Sophie, I never realised before. You look just like me.'

Sophie shrugged. ''Course. We're sisters, aren't we? Did anything else happen?'

'The best thing of all,' said Emma, pulling up her knees and hugging them. 'I came home by myself, cos Chris and Nick had soccer. I stopped at the corner where the pretty garden is, an' the lady was there. She asked me if I wanted to see her irises round the back. She said she knew I liked flowers because I always stopped to look at hers. She asked me if I had a garden of my own.'

'Well,' said Sophie, frowning as she looked around. 'This is a garden, I suppose.'

'Not a proper one,' Emma insisted. 'It's just weeds and overgrown things. It isn't…it isn't loved. But that doesn't matter because the lady said she'd give me some bits of plants and tell me how to make them grow.'

'Oh, Emma,' whispered Sophie, her eyes enormous. She pressed her hands against her throat.

'I know. And guess what. I told Mummy and she said…oh Sophie, she said she knows how to make a garden and she'll help me if I want.'

Sophie looked through the branches into the distance. She smiled but it wasn't really a happy smile, her eyes were too sad. 'You know, Emma,' she said quietly. 'Soon you won't need a Hiding Place. You're growing up. Changing. Soon you won't have time to come and talk to me.'

Emma stared hard at Sophie. 'Maybe,' she conceded at last. She began to sort through their pile of pebbles and leaves. 'Maybe, Sophie. But not yet. Not yet.'

Because of Rose

At first, it seemed as if Caroline coped well with the loss of the baby. Perhaps she was a little quieter, but she had always been given to long periods of introspection. That was one of the reasons that Harry loved her – the way she had somehow retained the innocence, the sense of wonder of a child. In the weeks following her miscarriage, Harry saw with relief the sweet dreaminess return to her face. She went about her household chores humming softly. He heard her laughter in the mornings as she dressed the little girls.

Now that spring had come, they spent most of their time in the garden and there was a great bustle of organising rubber boots and trowels and whose turn it was to ride in the wheelbarrow. When he came home from work, he was greeted with great excitement.

'Daddy, Daddy, come an' look. One of my 'nenomes is out and it's red.'

'I fed the sparrows.'

'So did I, and we think you ought to leave your crusts, Daddy. Mummy won't get cross with you and you don't need curls. Cos, Daddy, then we'd have lots more crumbs.'

Smiling at them all, it seemed to Harry that Caroline's face was just as bright and eager as the little girls', all of them children together. He felt a rush of gratitude. It was a pity about the baby, but such things happened. Anyway, Caroline was very young yet, barely twenty-six. Next year, perhaps, they could try again. Meanwhile, he was content with what he had.

Elizabeth, the eldest of his daughters, was six years old, with her mother's heart-shaped face and wide-set blue eyes. She had her mother's habit, too, of singing to herself, particularly when she was alone. But he recognised a strong practical common sense in her as well.

It amused and delighted him to realise in that way she was like him. He knew he was stolid and rather boring, so to see something of himself in this quicksilver child touched him deeply.

Hannah was five. She looked nothing like Elizabeth. Neither did she resemble her parents. She had a rather plain little face, large hazel eyes and a quantity of soft, straight brown hair. Harry worried a little about Hannah because she seemed so ordinary, but Caroline laughed at him.

'It's true she's not pretty like Elizabeth,' she said. 'But, don't you see, Harry, she's what they'll call interesting. And, besides, she's clever. She must take after you in that. Maybe she'll be a professor like you, or a lawyer, or a doctor.'

Harry protested. 'How can you possibly tell? She hasn't even started school.'

'Trust me, Harry. A mother always knows. Just you wait and see.' Caroline's eyes danced with a secret mischief. So Harry had to laugh too.

Sarah, two and a half, was still a baby, round-faced with a riot of silken curls.

'She's got charm,' announced Caroline. 'Everyone always stops me to talk to her when we're at the shops, and she smiles right back, reaching out her arms. I'm frightened she'll get spoilt with so much attention.'

'I don't think so,' Harry said, watching the children playing in the garden. 'She's just friendly. Though how she got that way, I don't know. You're so shy and I'm, well – I'm hardly gregarious.'

Caroline put her hands up to her throat. She turned to Harry, her eyes wet with sudden emotion. 'Oh, Harry, we are so lucky to have them. All so beautiful and…special. And now, of course, we've got Rose.'

'Rose?' repeated Harry, staring at her 'What do you mean, Rose?' He felt a premonition of disaster.

'Oh, Harry, honestly!' Caroline laughed and her laughter sounded just as light-hearted as the laughter of the children outside. 'We have to start calling the baby by her proper name. And it's such a pretty name. Old–fashioned, of course, but it suits her so well. She's just like a little pink rosebud all tucked up in her blankets.'

Harry couldn't think of anything to say. Perhaps it was best to say nothing. He walked away from the window and settled himself in his favourite chair with his newspaper.

Yet although weeks went by and Caroline made no further mention of Rose, Harry felt uncomfortable. Watching Caroline rocking in her chair, he could almost visualise the baby in her arms. Now he was alerted, he found other things to disturb him – a half-empty bottle of baby formula in the fridge, a pile of freshly laundered nappies, an empty tube of baby lotion in the garbage. Once, he awoke from a nightmare and was sure he could hear a baby crying. 'I'm going mad,' he thought. 'This can't be happening.'

But Caroline seemed exactly the same. The house was kept as immaculate as ever, the garden flourished, the little girls were well looked after. And Caroline's eyes were so calm. Surely, if there were something wrong, he would see it in her face. But she had the same sweet dreaminess, the same easy way of laughing. It was he who was changing, becoming nervous, suspicious.

He was almost glad when Caroline began to speak openly of Rose. He couldn't explain why, but he found it reassuring.

'Look, Harry, they had a sale at Driscoll's and I bought some material for the girls' summer dresses. See – this blue flowery stuff for Elizabeth and Sarah, because they're so fair, and this striped for Hannah and oh! isn't this lovely, this deep pink broderie anglaise for Rose. It will look so beautiful on her. Isn't it funny that she's so dark. Nothing like the other children at all.'

Harry found it hard to swallow and cleared his throat. To hide his confusion, he bent forward as if to examine the various materials.

Caroline watched him anxiously. 'You're not cross, are you, Harry, that I spent so much money? Rose's was particularly expensive because it's embroidered. But I only need such a little piece, she's so small yet, and she's never had anything new, just hand-me-downs from her sisters. Oh! she's going to look so sweet.'

Harry knew once and for all that he could do nothing to destroy her delusion. It would be cruel. He loved her too much. In any case, what difference did it really make? His world was secure. His wife was happy, the little girls safe and warm in bed. Surely, there was room for Rose as well.

'Of course I'm not cross, darling,' he said, putting his arm around Caroline. 'Spend what you like. I only wish you'd get something to make up for yourself.'

Now that he accepted Rose, he felt a curious light–heartedness. Everything was all right. If sometimes he woke after a disturbing dream, he told himself that next year, perhaps, Caroline would be pregnant again and, once she had a real baby to care for, Rose would fade away and be forgotten. Even when the little girls started talking about Rose, he made no protest.

'Sssh, Sarah – you know Mummy said we must be quiet. Rose is asleep.'

'Sarah's in the sandpit with Rose. She always plays with Rose now.'

'Yeah, I know, but it's because Sarah and Rose are the little ones and you an' me, Hannah, are the big ones.'

'Let's find that big ball, Sarah, and roll it along the floor to Rose. She loves that and she looks so cute when she claps her hands.'

There was no way Harry could have prevented the tragedy. It was the kind of thing that happened to other people. At first, he could not take it in. He returned, unexpectedly early from an interstate conference, to find their house had been gutted by fire. He stood staring stupidly at the blackened, silent ruins. Ashes drifted in the wind and he thought at first that was what caused the bitter taste in his mouth. A kindly neighbour came and told him the name of the hospital where his family had been taken.

When he got there, they took him to the room where Caroline was. He hardly heard what they were saying. Just a confusion of noise in the background. In his mind, he could only hear the devouring flames and the screams of his children.

Caroline lay facing the wall, her hands grotesquely bandaged. When he spoke her name, she turned to him, her eyes wide with terror. 'Oh, Harry, Harry,' she whispered. She began to whimper like a beaten child. 'I tried to save them all and I nearly did. I got Elizabeth and Hannah out. But Sarah… It was because of saving Rose that I couldn't get Sarah out in time.' She began sobbing wildly, flinging herself about on the bed like someone insane.

Harry tried to protest but the words stuck in his throat. There was nothing he could say. He had lost everything. He asked to see Elizabeth and Hannah and, full of compassion, they led him away.

Losing Laura

When she was forty-three years old and had been married for more than twenty years, Eleanor gave birth to her first child. As soon as they left her alone with the baby, she examined it carefully – the little hands and feet, pink as the inside of a shell, the head of soft dark hair, the exquisite tiny ears. It wasn't what she had expected. She turned her head away and looked through the window where the early morning light was just beginning to outline the trees and shrubs of the hospital garden. 'You're not what I wanted,' she whispered. 'You're not Laura.'

She had never told anyone about Laura. She had watched her friends, one after the other, with their babies and she had choked back her bitterness. 'One day,' she told herself. 'One day it will be me.' The baby she so desperately wanted took shape in her mind, fair-haired, blue-eyed, always dressed in white. It was a comfort to her. Her Laura. When her friend Georgina had twins, a girl and a boy, she was able to congratulate her wholeheartedly because Laura stood next to her, her little hand in her mother's, her curls tied back with pink ribbon, her eyes wide with wonder as she admired the babies.

At home, in the lonely afternoons when all the housework was done, Laura sat with her as she did her embroidery, arms around her knees, lips parted while her mother told her stories. And as her friends' children grew into adolescence so too did Laura – a slim young girl who moved with an old-fashioned grace, her eyes soft with dreams. When Enid confided how worried she was about Julie, Eleanor smiled secretly because of course her Laura didn't go to wild parties or experiment with drugs or expect to bring her boyfriend home for the night. Laura arranged the flowers in the dining room and read romantic poetry. When it was hot, she went for long walks in the park, her sweet little face shielded by a wide-brimmed hat. Laura was the kind of daughter every woman wanted.

'And she's mine,' whispered Eleanor, hugging herself. 'All mine. And they don't know.'

She never even told Jonathan. But he was her father. He knew. Eleanor liked to think Laura was a secret between them, all the more poignant because they had never talked about her.

When the doctor confirmed her pregnancy, Eleanor was incredulous. 'I'm too old,' she said, shaking her head. 'I'm sure I'm not ready for this.'

The doctor had laughed. She had been consulting him for years. He knew, as no one else did, how much she had longed for a child. 'It's a bit of a shock, isn't it? Give yourself time to get used to it.' He patted her on the shoulder. 'Congratulations. Now you go home and tell Jonathan.'

'But…but…' Eleanor clutched at her handbag. 'My friend, Enid… her boy…she's about to become a grandmother. How on earth will I manage…a little baby? I mean…'

'You'll manage,' the doctor said complacently. 'It's your dream come true.'

And so it seemed. Her cheeks flushed, her eyes bright, Eleanor looked like a young girl when she told Jonathan. He put down his newspaper and regarded her, bemused. 'Well, well,' he smiled. 'It's what we've always hoped for. A child. And all the better because we've had to wait so long. We're ready for it now, don't you think, Ellie? I mean, look at us – we're financially secure, established, one might say, got this beautiful home… oh! it couldn't have happened at a better time.'

'But,' faltered Eleanor, 'we're so old.'

'Old!' Jonathan laughed. 'Of course we're not old. And anyway this'll keep us young forever. When all our friends are thinking of retirement, you and I and our son' – he glanced at Eleanor's face and quickly amended – 'or daughter, whatever, we'll be planning holidays, trips to the beach, the zoo… Good gracious, I haven't been to the zoo for thirty years, but now…' He laughed again. 'Oh, Eleanor, this is the most wonderful news. I feel like a boy again.' He waltzed her around the room until they both collapsed on the chesterfield, their arms around one another.

But later that night, when Eleanor was preparing for bed, she felt anxious again. 'Oh, Laura,' she whispered. But Laura wasn't there any more. No slim girl-figure stepped out of the shadows. Eleanor felt a chill of premonition. 'Nonsense,' she told herself. 'Of course Laura isn't here. Laura is…' She put her hands on her stomach. 'I just have to wait. Tomorrow I'll begin the layette. I'll make it all myself – little smocked nightgowns, lacy dresses, matinee jackets and I'll embroider them all with grub roses. It's hard to find silk thread nowadays but I'll manage. Oh, nine months won't be long enough. I have so much to do.' She fell asleep smiling.

Sometimes, though, in the long winter afternoons as she sat sewing, Eleanor was apprehensive. What if something went wrong? What if Laura were still-born? But her continuing good health belied her doubts. She had never felt better. Her hair, her skin – she glowed with her pregnancy.

'You're so lucky,' said Enid, visiting. 'Not even morning sickness. No one would believe we were the same age.'

Eleanor laughed softly and showed her friend the shawl she was crocheting. It was as delicate as spider web.

'I've never seen anything so beautiful,' said Enid.

'I've taken a lot of trouble over it,' Eleanor said, smiling. 'But my baby, my little girl…well, I want everything to be perfect for her.'

'What if it's a boy? Doesn't Jonathan want a son?'

Eleanor frowned but Enid was bent over the shawl and didn't notice.

'It won't be a boy,' said Eleanor, but her voice was thin and high and echoed unnecessarily in the sunny room.

'Well,' Eleanor said now to the baby. 'I was right about that, wasn't I? You're not a boy. Although maybe it would have been better if you had been. At least then Jonathan would have what he wanted.'

The baby yawned and stretched. It opened its eyes to stare at its mother. Its eyes were dark and unfocused. They made Eleanor feel uncomfortable.

'You don't like me either, do you?' she whispered, disconcerted. 'But I don't care. You can like whom you choose. One thing's for sure' – she put the baby down on the bed next to her and turned away from it – 'you're not having her name.'

When Jonathan came that afternoon, looking slightly ridiculous in his best suit and carrying a huge bouquet of flowers, he asked Eleanor what she was going to call the baby. He didn't seem upset it was a girl. He crooned over the little pink bundle like a fool, thought Eleanor critically. She felt a little jealous. He had barely glanced at her. She reached over to her bedside locker and got out her manicure set. She began carefully polishing her nails. 'I can't think of a name,' she said. 'Why don't you choose something?'

'But…but…surely you… I mean, you're her mother… It's your right and, besides, you'll think of something much prettier than I can… I don't know anything about little girls and…'

'Well,' Eleanor said, not looking at him, 'you're going to have to learn, aren't you? I mean, she's here now. It's not like we can give her back.'

Jonathan stared at her, confused.

All at once, Eleanor felt ashamed. She reached up and patted his cheek. 'You choose something,' she said softly. 'I'd really like it if you named her.'

'Well,' began Jonathan, 'well, we could call her after my mother, Isobel Mary. I'd, I'd like that.' He paused a moment. 'You don't think that's too old-fashioned, do you? I mean, we wouldn't want her to feel different. It'll be hard enough for her as it is, us being so much older than the parents of her friends.'

Eleanor glanced at him. He seemed to be contradicting all he had said before. But it didn't matter. Isobel Mary was as good a name as any. Appropriate, really. She hadn't liked Jonathan's mother. An autocratic old lady, determined to make trouble between them. Jonathan had been her only son… Of course, she had been dead for years. Just as well. It looked as if Jonathan were going to be a doting father. She didn't need an interfering grandmother as well…

Suddenly, Eleanor's facade of indifference crumbled. She turned her face to the wall and wept silently. 'Oh, Laura, Laura,' she whispered, pushing her knuckles into her mouth, 'what has happened to you? Where are you?'

The doctor diagnosed post-natal depression. Eleanor didn't bother to contradict him. She took the tablets he prescribed and tried to pretend an interest in the baby. Not that she had to see that much of her. Jonathan hired a competent nanny. Eleanor refused to let Isobel wear any of the clothes she had prepared. Jonathan protested at first but the nanny quickly reassured him.

'Lot of extra work all those frills and lace,' she told him. 'Pretty, yes, but hardly practical. No, what we need are some of those little jumpsuits.

They come in lovely bright colours and so easy to keep nice, too. You just leave it to me. I know what's right for our little darling. No sense in upsetting your poor wife, the way she is. You let her keep her beautiful things. Isobel will never know the difference.'

And Isobel didn't. She grew into a sturdy, cheerful little girl with wide-set hazel eyes, straight brown hair and a talent for mischief. Nanny dressed her in boys' overalls and little lace-up boots.

Jonathan was besotted with her. 'Isn't she a picture!' he said enthusiastically to Eleanor as he watched the little girl playing in the garden.

It was autumn and she was scuffling in the fallen leaves, lifting up her laughing little face to Nanny, her cheeks stung red with the wind.

Eleanor didn't answer. She wanted to cry out, 'What about Laura?' but she knew Jonathan wouldn't know what she was talking about. Forget, she whispered, I've got to forget about Laura…

One night, when Nanny was out, Eleanor was forced to go into Isobel because of her crying. Eleanor had hoped that, if she ignored it as usual, Jonathan would get up. But he only switched on the light and said, 'Bring her in here, Ellie. We'll let her sleep in with us. I know Nanny won't approve, but just this once won't hurt.'

Looking into his face, Eleanor felt a rush of compassion. Jonathan deserved better than this. She would get the child and let her share their bed. Surely, for one night, she could pretend they were a happy family.

Isobel was standing up in her cot, sobbing. When she saw her mother, she held up her arms. Eleanor picked her up. The baby nestled against her. She smelt of talcum powder and warm milk, her hair was silky soft… thistledown, thought Eleanor, thistledown on a summer's day. Tentatively, she wound a strand around her finger.

As if in a dream, Eleanor stumbled over to the rocking chair and sank down. 'Oh, Isobel,' she whispered, 'if only…' She shook her head. Something in her heart shuddered and she put her hand up to hold it still, 'Oh, Isobel, do you know where Laura is, where she went? I need her, oh I need her so much and you…you need her too because then…'

But Isobel's eyes, wide and strange, looked beyond her into the shadows.

Eleanor sighed. Hardly aware of what she was doing, she began to rock backwards and forwards. Isobel's eyelids fluttered and she put her thumb in her mouth. After a while, Eleanor got up and put her back in her cot.

But at the doorway she hesitated. She didn't want to leave Isobel. Holding her, rocking her, she had felt…something, whispered Eleanor, I felt… It was almost as if Laura were with us…as if Laura approved…

And in the morning Laura came back. Just like that. Only…only Laura was different. She was a little girl again, just a few years older than Isobel, but her eyes… It was as if, while she had been away, she had found out things and these things had saddened her. A waif, thought Eleanor, her throat constricting, she looks like a waif and I…

Quickly she took Laura's hand and led her over to the playpen, where Isobel was examining a tattered teddy bear. 'This is your baby sister,' she said. 'She…she's called Isobel and…'

Laura knelt down next to the playpen, her eyes questioning, her delicate little brows drawn together in a frown. But then, all of a sudden, she smiled and Eleanor laughed with relief.

And everything was all right. Together, Laura and her mother redesigned the garden. 'Isobel needs a place to play,' Laura explained. So they fenced off a section and provided her with a sandpit and a collection of buckets and spades. 'Maybe a watering can?' suggested Laura. 'It's summer now. It wouldn't matter if she got a bit wet, would it, Mummy?'

But Laura wouldn't play with Isobel. 'I belong to you, Mummy,' she said. She helped set out the petunia seedlings while Isobel dug happily in the sand, her sun hat half off, one strap of her overalls undone and dangling down her back.

Laura sat back on her heels. 'We have to be kind to Isobel, don't we, Mummy, because she's my sister.'

Eleanor put down her trowel. A startling thought leapt into her mind. Maybe Laura didn't really like Isobel. Maybe Laura wanted her to hurt Isobel. But Laura's eyes were innocent and very steadfast. Eleanor felt ashamed.

Relieved that Eleanor was so much better, Jonathan eventually replaced Nanny with a part-time housekeeper. 'Just to help out with the cooking and cleaning,' he explained. 'No sense in you wearing yourself out. You just concentrate on looking after Isobel. Now that she's at kindergarten, you'll have the mornings free and she'll be company for you in the afternoons.'

Eleanor nodded. She refurnished the living room. She and Laura spent a long time choosing the drapes – roses on a soft grey background. 'Not that your father or even Isobel will notice,' Eleanor said, laughing. 'Two of a kind, they are.'

Laura smiled. 'Like us, Mummy. We're two of a kind, aren't we?'

Eleanor hugged her. 'Yes, darling. Of course we are.'

'I want plaits,' insisted Isobel one morning, soon after she started school. 'Curls are silly.'

Eleanor put down the curling wand and stared at her. 'But Laura has curls.'

Isobel tossed her head and looked away. And Eleanor had to admit plaits suited her. 'She's not at all pretty,' she thought dispassionately, looking at her daughter's round, freckled little face with its too wide eyes and determined mouth. 'I might as well let her have her hair the way she wants. It will certainly save time.'

When she was six years old, Isobel demanded a pony.

'A pony,' exclaimed Jonathan. 'Whatever next!'

But Eleanor said, 'Oh, Isobel, surely not. We have nowhere to keep it. Wouldn't you rather have ballet lessons?'

'No,' said Isobel, glaring at her mother.

Eleanor bit her lip. She couldn't say anything about Laura with Jonathan there but that night, when she was helping Isobel get ready for bed, she tried to tell the little girl how much Laura liked ballet. 'I could get you pink slippers tied with ribbon like hers and…'

Isobel went over to her mirror and started brushing her hair. 'I'm tired of hearing about Laura,' she said. 'She sounds stupid. I don't see why I should have to do the things she likes.'

'Because…' Eleanor began.

Isobel put down her brush. Her mouth was trembling and she jerked her head away. 'You like her more than you like me,' she whispered. 'You don't like me at all.'

'No, I…'

Isobel got into bed. Her face was closed. Stricken, Eleanor stumbled from the room.

Jonathan and Isobel reached a compromise. 'Riding lessons until you're eight and then we'll see.' So every Saturday, all togged out in jodhpurs and a hard hat, Isobel went off with Jonathan to the local riding school. Laura and Eleanor watched them go.

'It's so hot,' said Laura, wrinkling her nose. 'I don't know how she can be bothered. She comes back so dirty, too.' She slipped a hand in her mother's. 'Aren't you glad you've got me, Mummy, to do quiet things with?'

Eleanor turned. 'Oh, darling,' she cried, 'I don't know what I'd do without you. I mean…' Her voice dropped to a whisper. 'Laura…Laura, you'll never go away again will you? Before, when you… Oh, Laura, I couldn't bear it if…'

Laura looked into the distance. She sighed. She got up and crossed the lawn to the rose garden. Eleanor watched as she carefully broke off a rosebud. 'I like these pink ones,' she said. 'I like them best. You do too, don't you, Mummy? You like the pink ones best too, don't you?' Eleanor leaned forward and, very gently, touched the rosebud in Laura's hand. She did not know what the little girl was trying to tell her.

One Sunday, Jonathan suggested they go for a picnic by the river. 'We could hire a boat,' he said. 'You'd like that wouldn't you, Isobel?'

Eleanor wasn't at all sure she wanted to go. But Jonathan and Isobel's excitement was contagious.

Even Laura was enthusiastic. 'We can always sit on the bank and watch if it's too hot for rowing, Mummy.' she said. She helped Eleanor find the esky and pack the chicken and salad for lunch.

'We might go fishing,' said Jonathan. 'You'd like that wouldn't you, Isobel? Catch our own fish and fry them up like the cavemen, eh?'

An hour later, they were at the riverside, car parked under a convenient tree, table set up with the esky, banana lounge waiting for Eleanor.

'I won't go rowing,' she told Jonathan and Isobel as they set off on foot to hire a boat. 'I'll just sit here with my book and be a spectator when you come round the bend.'

She leaned back, her eyes half-closed. The light danced on the water. She could hear in the distance Isobel's high, excited voice. She smiled. It was so peaceful. Laura wandered along the bank, picking wild-flowers and singing to herself. Somewhere a kookaburra began to laugh.

'I'm so lucky,' thought Eleanor, contentedly, her mind beginning to drift.

Suddenly she was startled awake. Jonathan was standing up in a rowing boat, waving his arms wildly and shouting. The boat rocked dangerously. Whatever was he doing? If he weren't careful, he'd have the boat over and then…

A bird swooped by her. Eleanor stared after it, confused. A dark bird, its wings black against the sun. That was odd, the light was so bright. Before…before, everything had been soft with shadows. And Laura, where was Laura? She had been playing on the riverbank, Eleanor had warned her not to go too far away. It wasn't like Laura to be disobedient. Perhaps… Eleanor frowned.

There was a sudden splash as Jonathan dived into the water. Eleanor jumped to her feet. What did it mean…the empty boat…the turbulent water…the bright light. And the bird, the bird. Laura, where was Laura? What had happened to her? The bird had been so dark and…

Jonathan staggered up the bank. He was carrying something. Something heavy. A child. She could see its head of soft, dark hair, its white limbs. They were drooping over Jonathan's arms. Eleanor put her hand to her mouth. A little girl. Jonathan had dived into the water to save a little girl. All at once she felt a dreadful pain in her chest. My heart, she thought, distracted. No, it's a bird, a bird is trying to break free from my heart. I can feel its beak, its claws tearing as it struggles. Oh, poor bird, poor trapped bird, I…

Jonathan was shouting. His voice was so loud. Eleanor turned to him. He was shouting at her. 'For God's sake, Eleanor, do something. Don't just stand there. Run for help. Run, you bloody fool, run.'

Eleanor took a deep breath. When she looked at Jonathan again, it was as if everything had suddenly come into focus. She felt very calm. Jonathan had rescued a little girl from the water. But that wasn't enough. She had to do something too. CPR. She knew how to do CPR. She had to do CPR, otherwise the little girl…

'Put her down,' she said, moving purposefully forward. 'That's right. Tilt her head back.' She knelt down next to the child. 'You go, Jonathan. Ring for an ambulance at the kiosk where you got the boat. They'll have a phone. Hurry up. It's no good watching me. I don't need your help. I know what to do.'

After a few moments, the little girl gave a choking splutter, struggled to lift her head and was violently sick. Eleanor helped her sit up. 'It's all right,' she said, brushing the damp hair from her face. 'Oh, Laura, you gave me such a fright. I thought I'd lost you. I thought…'

'Laura?' interrupted the little girl. 'What are you calling me Laura for, Mummy? I'm not Laura. I'm Isobel.'

Eleanor looked at her carefully. 'Isobel.' She gave an unsteady laugh. 'Whatever have I been thinking of? Isobel. Of course it's Isobel. But it doesn't matter, does it? Not now. Oh, Isobel, you're all right. Just as long as you're all right.' She hugged Isobel to her, her lips against her hair.

Above the little girl's head, she could see the river bank, the boat bobbing on the quiet water, the trailing willow branches, each leaf outlined in gold. A long time ago, Laura had been playing there, her curls tied back with pink ribbon, her hands full of wildflowers…or had she… Eleanor could no longer be certain. Laura had been a dream. She had always been a dream and now she no longer mattered.

'My baby,' whispered Eleanor, her arms around Isobel. 'My baby.'

from *Children at the Gate*

'… Will the veiled sister pray
For children at the gate
who will not go away and cannot pray.'
T.S. Eliot, 'Ash Wednesday'

Dark Gods of the Woods

On Saturday afternoons they're free. That's what Therese says. Olivia and Helen know what she means. Monday to Friday is school and homework and endless piano practice and Sunday is church. Even Saturday morning's all taken up with helping Mum, hanging out the washing and tidying their bedroom and vacuuming.

'I thought lunchtime would never come,' says Olivia, flinging herself down under the ash tree with her sisters. 'Mum made me dust the things on the mantelpiece twice. She reckoned I'd just flicked at them the first time.'

'She's probably right,' says Therese, unimpressed. 'I've seen the way you do things.'

Olivia drops her head and busies herself with the folds of her skirt.

'What'll we do today, Terry?' says Helen quickly. 'What have you got planned?'

Olivia's the oldest but that's not important. Therese is the leader.

Therese waits a moment before she answers. She leans back, her hands under her head, staring at the sky through squinted eyes. Then she smiles. 'I thought we'd go down and have a good look at the old hay shed. Possibilities, it's got possibilities that place. We ought to check it out.'

'But…but…' protests Helen. 'We're not allowed to. You know that. Dad said, Dad said when he let Mr Fraser have the bit of land there to grow vegetables, he said we weren't to go there and play. He said we weren't to bother Mr Fraser because…'

Therese ignores her. She turns instead to Olivia. 'What about you, Liv?' she says deliberately. 'You coming or are you staying here with Helen?'

Before Olivia can answer, Helen says, hot-cheeked, 'I never said I wasn't coming. I only said…'

'Well, then, what are we waiting for? Come on.'

Olivia hangs back. She bites her lip. 'But what about Mr Fraser?' she whispers. 'I don't like him. He…'

'He won't be there. He's never there on Saturdays. He goes to the pub instead. That's why he hasn't any money. He spends it all at the pub.'

Olivia feels her throat tighten. 'Emmie Fraser's in my class. Last term I sat next to her. She's nice…'

'So? What's that got to do with it? I never said anything about her, did I? Come on.'

Single-file they go through the orchard. Olivia likes it there. The trees are so friendly, not like the scrub trees that are dark and unpredictable and have secrets they won't share. She puts out her hand and touches the trunk of an apple tree as she passes. The last of its leaves flutter like little yellow banners.

Without waiting for her sisters' help, Therese wrenches open the cocky-gate and they're in the paddock. The grass, left over from summer, is waist high. It rustles uneasily in the wind.

Olivia frowns. Her father is no farmer. He's neglected the land. Even Mr Fraser, even if he drinks too much, he's doing something, he's got his patch of vegetables, they're all tangled up with weeds, but it's still something. Something real. While her father, her respectable father, has hidden himself in his books.

Helen and Therese have gone over to the hay shed. Olivia runs after them. It's quite empty.

Therese looks around. 'Just what I thought,' she says, pleased. 'Perfect. We can make this into our place, our secret place and every Saturday we can come here and play.'

But Olivia's still standing in the doorway. 'I…'she begins. 'The reason Dad told us not to come here's got nothing to do with Mr Fraser,' she says slowly. 'That's just an excuse. They…they found someone here last year. A man. He was dead. He climbed up there where that platform is and hanged himself. He…'

Therese turns around, startled. 'Don't be ridiculous. You're making it up.'

'No, I heard Dad tell Mr Fraser. Anyway, it's true. I can feel it.'

'Feel it! As if! Get real. Come on, Helen. Let's climb up. I'll give you a leg up if you want.'

But Helen, wide-eyed, shakes her head. 'No. No, I don't want to. Livvie's right. I don't like it here. It's creepy. Let's go back.'

Therese stamps her foot. 'Creepy! You're a baby, Helen. And who cares? Who cares if he killed himself? He isn't here now, is he? Oh! It's not fair. You two! You spoil everything. All week I've planned what we could do. Once we got onto that platform, we could reach the roof easy. Just think what we'd be able to see once we got onto the roof.'

Olivia says quickly, placatingly, stretching out a hand to lay it on her sister's arm. 'Terry, I never said I wouldn't, and Helen will if I will, won't you, Lennie? We…'

But it's no good. Therese flings back her hair. Her eyes are fierce. 'I know what you said,' she says bitterly. 'You've spoiled it, Olivia. You always do. I don't know why I bother with you. You've spoiled it for all of us.' Her voice breaks. She turns and marches out of the shed, her head held high, her shoulders rigid.

Olivia and Helen follow her in silence. After a while, Helen slips her hand into her sister's. She's crying but Olivia, tactfully, pretends not to notice.

Therese climbs under the fence. She's going down to the creek. It's not their creek; it's Mr Reynold's. He's not like Dad. His land is important to him; he doesn't like trespassers. Olivia and Helen don't say anything, though. They follow Therese through the undergrowth, a tangle of blackberries and gorse and bracken. Olivia stops by a fallen tree. It's decorated with lichen and she puts out a hand and touches it tentatively. It's like lace. Gold lace, she whispers and the idea pleases her so much she loses sight of the others and Helen has to come back to find her.

Suddenly Therese holds up her hand. 'Look at that,' she hisses. She's herself again. They can hear it in her voice.

The tension goes out of Olivia and she laughs. 'Mushrooms.'

'Not mushrooms, stupid. Toadstools. Fungi.' Therese bends down to pick one. Her face is dreamy. 'Toadstools are magic.' The toadstool, thin-stalked, almost translucent, lies in her hand. It quivers like something alive. There's an aura around it, a golden aura.

'Toadstools are poisonous,' begins Helen. 'At school Miss Martin said…' She catches Therese's eye and subsides into silence.

Therese smiles to herself. 'We should make an altar,' she says slowly. 'We should make an altar and offer these toadstools to the gods of the woods, the dark gods of the woods.'

'But…' Olivia doesn't like the way Therese is looking at her. The gods, the dark gods Therese is talking about, they are looking at her out of her sister's eyes. She shudders and turns away.

'All right, then,' says Therese suddenly brisk. 'I'll build the altar. You two go and find other things, other things worthy to sacrifice.'

Helen scurries away obediently and, after a moment, Olivia follows. But she doesn't look properly. She can't. Her heart is beating too fast. All she finds is a bird's feather and a little glittering stone. Helen's more successful. She's got a handful of late blackberries, a fern frond and two or three fluffy gum-nut blossoms.

'Good,' says Therese, smiling approval. In their absence, she's built a clumsy altar of stone and small branches. 'Put your offerings down now. You first, Helen. The gods are pleased with you.' When it's Olivia's turn, she makes no comment but her eyes are cold. Her lip curls a little. She can't quite hide her contempt.

The blood rushes into Olivia's cheeks. She knows suddenly that, whatever she does, Therese will always feel like that. Contemptuous. It's not enough for Therese to be their leader. She wants to be the eldest as well.

Then it's Therese's turn. Kneeling, she makes a bouquet of the toadstools and places them in the centre. Then she stands back. She lifts her hands high above her head and walks slowly around the altar. When she stops, she extends her arm so the others can see, around her wrist, the gold charm bracelet she got for her last birthday. Her head flung back, her eyes closed, she snatches with her other hand and wrenches it free.

Olivia catches her breath. It's very quiet, too quiet, but in the silence she thinks she hears the bracelet, breaking, cry out and its voice is thin and high like the voice of a little girl. Therese holds it a moment above the altar, then smiling, she lets it slide slowly through her fingers until it falls at last among the other offerings.

'There,' says Therese. 'There. It's done.' She whirls to face them. 'I have sacrificed the most. The gods will choose me. Now hold hands. We will say the prayer.'

Olivia's mouth is dry. She tries to meet her sister's gaze without flinching but she can't. Defeated, she takes Helen's hand and lets Therese take hers.

Therese tilts back her head and laughs. Her face, uplifted, is very pale. It quivers with light. 'Hear,' she shouts. 'Hear, all you gods of darkness. Hear our prayer. Accept our sacrifices. Give us of your power. Fit us for...'

'No.' Suddenly Olivia snatches her hand away. 'No, I don't want...' She stops.

Therese is glaring at her. Her eyes are wide and dark and quite, quite mad. 'Take Helen's hand,' she says very quietly. 'Take Helen's hand, Olivia, and mine.' She pauses. 'If you don't, I swear, I swear to you, we will never play with you again. Never. I mean it.'

'Livvie...' falters Helen but Therese quells her with a look.

'Go on, Olivia. Do what I say. Or...'

Olivia can't look at either of them. Her hands twist themselves together as if they have a will of their own and she struggles to keep them still. 'No,' she says. 'I can't. It's wrong. You don't know what you might make happen. Or...or maybe you do and...' She glances around her. It's so quiet. The gods, the gods of darkness, she thinks, they're waiting for my answer, they're waiting for me to... She says again, amazed at the strength of her own voice, 'This is a stupid game, Therese. We shouldn't be here anyway. I'm going home.'

Helen starts to cry.

Therese turns on her furiously. 'Shut up. Shut up you imbecile,' and her hand flies out and she slaps Helen hard. When her hand comes away, there's a red patch on Helen's face. Slowly, painfully, the colour rises in her own cheeks till it looks as if someone has slapped her too. She turns to face Olivia. Her lips are quivering and her eyes are her own again but Olivia doesn't say anything. 'Livvie,' whispers Therese, holding out her hands. 'Livvie, I didn't mean it. I...'

Olivia takes no notice. She's staring at the sky through the canopy of leaves. It's as if she's forgotten them. She starts to smile. Somewhere, far off, a bird begins to sing and her eyes widen and go dreamy. 'Sweet,' she whispers. 'Oh, how sweet.' Then, her head tilted to one side, she starts to climb the slope, following the sound until she's lost from sight behind a scramble of gums and bracken.

With a little incoherent cry, Therese runs to the altar to retrieve her broken bracelet.

Lisa Had Brown Eyes

The dreams about Lisa start when I get home. I've spent the last few years with my grandparents. My father insisted on it when he found out how bad it was with my mother. But she's better now. Or at least that's what she says. She wrote and begged me to come back. Everyone tried to talk me out of it but she's my mother; I owe her something. Loyalty. Another chance. Love even. Maybe I just want to stop feeling guilty. Some secrets are best not kept. I should have told my father earlier about her drinking.

Maybe that's what reminds me of Lisa. She had secrets too. I wonder now about the other girls: Helen, who was always laughing, and Julieanne and Natalie. Perhaps they had things to hide as well. I'm glad I don't know. It's bad enough knowing about Lisa.

Lisa started high school the same time as us. That's the Lisa I want to remember. She's got slim, tanned legs, a short pleated skirt; her fine honey-coloured hair swings free around her shoulders.

'She washes it in lemon juice, you know,' says Julieanne, pursing up her mouth. 'She hopes that'll make it go blonde.'

'She doesn't wash it enough,' retorts Natalie, pushing back her own shining hair. 'By Friday it looks disgusting. So greasy.'

'Oh, well.' Julieanne shrugs. 'That's not really her fault. Her mother's awfully strict. She won't let her wash it more than once a week.'

'How do you know that?' asks Helen.

Lisa didn't go to our primary school so we don't know anything about her.

'Her mother's on the hospital committee with mine. She's foreign. Lithuanian. Ukrainian. Something weird like that. She's always going on about Lisa. It's gets on Mum's nerves.'

I keep quiet. I'm not really part of the group but they put up with me. They have to. They've known me since kindergarten.

During lessons I watch Lisa. I watch everyone. I draw pictures in the margin of my schoolbooks – a kingfisher in flight to represent Julieanne, a tussock of spiky grass for Natalie, an iridescent butterfly for Helen. I smile as I outline it in coloured pencil. Helen is such fun, with her curls and dimples and round, freckled face. Even the teachers like her. I wish she were my real friend. I glance across at Lisa. I chew the end of my pencil and frown. Then I know. Lisa is a pool of brown water with the sun shining on it. She catches my eye and gives me a sudden smile. Perhaps that's why I like her. She treats me like an equal.

But I'm not really friends with her. Not then. I stick with the group. I'm not brave enough to be different. Sometimes, though, I do things with her. We practise shooting goals for netball, compare maths homework; I even help her learn her catechism because she's going to be confirmed.

'Mummy's making my dress,' she confides. 'It's white lace and she's embroidered it with seed pearls, lilies of the valley, all around the hem.'

I turn away. My mother would never do anything like that for me. Perhaps that's part of Lisa's attraction. She represents all the things I want but can't have.

The next year, Lisa's in a different class and it's not until Year Eleven that we find ourselves doing the same subjects. I'm glad when Lisa asks if she can sit next to me. Most of the other kids are boys and I don't know any of them. Oh, I know their names all right, but not the people behind the faces. Names are like faces, just masks. Sometimes I think I don't know anyone, not even myself. Perhaps it's because everyone has changed so much. Faces that used to be round and childish and eager are thinner, eyes wary; even hair once left alone is disciplined, styled. Not mine of course. Mine is still long and the fringe I've cut in the front is crooked and hangs in my eyes.

'Most of the time your hair is all over the place and you look a mess,' Julieanne tells me. 'But sometimes, like today, it all comes together and you look ethereal.' She sounds surprised.

I bend down to retie my shoelace so she can't see how pleased I am.

Then her voice hardens. 'It isn't fair. Your face is wasted on you. You don't even care. Now, if I had it, I'd use it. It'd be an advantage. But you – you're hopeless.' She gives me a sudden violent push that she pretends is friendly.

Julieanne doesn't like me. She never has. I don't know why she still insists we walk home together.

Lisa is like me. She doesn't look any different. Her tanned face, her fine hair that hangs to her shoulders like silk, brown silk shot with gold, her smile. They haven't changed. She's even got the same look of eager expectancy. She's sure the world is a good place. It frightens me. The one thing I'm certain of is the darkness of man's heart. That's a phrase I got from William Golding's *Lord of the Flies*. It explains so much. I recite it to myself like a mantra. It fills me with pity.

Lisa confides in me about her mother. 'She's had a terrible life. Her parents were refugees after the war, you know. She wants me to have all the things she didn't when she was growing up.' Her eyes search my face. 'It's difficult, you know. I'm grateful but... It's like she wants to be me.' She looks down and her hair falls forward like a curtain. 'I don't want the same things. I want...' Her voice is just a whisper. I can hardly hear her. 'I don't know who I am, me or Mummy.'

I think she's crying but I can't be sure, because her hair hides her face. The other girls laugh when they hear her call her mother 'Mummy' but I don't. I wish my mother was the kind you could call 'Mummy' even when you were nearly sixteen years old.

Lisa tells me about Scott too. He's her boyfriend. He's already at university, so I've never met him of course, but I don't like the sound of him. He sounds sort of off-hand. I don't think Lisa knows much about people. And she wants too much. She wants to make up for her mother's lonely childhood. Most of all, she wants Scott to love her. I try to warn her but she just shakes her head and laughs. 'You'll find out, Rhiannon. One day you'll have a boyfriend too and...'

My lips are stiff. 'I don't think so.'

'Why not? You shouldn't be so shy.' She reaches out and pushes my hair back from my face. 'You're pretty, Rhiannon, really pretty.' Her eyes are very soft. 'I promise you, Rhiannon, it will happen.'

I turn away. I'm trembling and I don't want her to notice. But my feelings for her change then. I start to care about her.

'My mother doesn't like Scott,' Lisa explains. 'She says he's unsuitable and she tries to stop me seeing him. She...' Her voice falters. 'She... oh, Rhiannon, she lies. She tells him I'm not home when he rings and... and...yesterday she told him I was out with Mark Boulger.'

'Oh, Lisa.'

She swallows. 'I don't know what to do. I've written to him but…
What if he believes her… What if…?'

I try to reassure her. 'He'll know it isn't true. He knows how you feel
about him.'

'But it's different with boys. You don't understand. He…he wants me
to sleep with him. He keeps on about it. Do you think, if I do, it will sort
of prove…'

'I don't think you ought to. I mean not unless…' I feel my cheeks get
hot.

Lisa gets impatient then. 'Oh, Rhiannon, you're such a child. What
would you know? All the things people say about you are true.'

I let my hair fall over my face. It's a trick I learned from her. I want
to get up and run away. The front lawn, shaded by a line of poplar trees,
is dotted with little groups of kids eating their lunches, all talking, all
laughing, all… Desperately I start to pluck at the grass.

Lisa says, 'I'm sorry. I didn't mean that.' She touches my hand.
'Please,' she says. 'Please don't get upset. I only meant…well, you are
different from everyone else. You know that.' She hesitates. 'I'm glad you
are. Really.'

I won't look at her. 'You're right.' I whisper. 'I don't know anything
about boys. I can't tell you what to do. I just think, well, I wouldn't.'

Lisa sighs. 'It'll be all right.' She gives a little laugh. 'It'll have to be. I
won't let Mother spoil it.'

I think, she has lost something. From Mummy to Mother. The other
girls have managed a compromise. They have Mum. For years, ever since
my father left, I have refused to call my mother anything.

More and more, Lisa becomes preoccupied with her mother. 'She
reads my diary,' she tells me. She blushes. 'She found out about Scott
and me, that we…that we slept together and… Oh, Rhiannon don't look
at me like that. I had to prove to him that I… Anyway, that's not the
important thing. She…' Her voice drops to a whisper. 'She's going to tell
my father. She says that if I ever see Scott again, she'll write to my father
and he'll have him charged because I'm under age.'

I stare at her. 'Your father?' I repeat. Lisa has never mentioned him
before. I got the impression he didn't live with them, that he'd left years
ago, that he was like mine.

'My father's in the navy. He's overseas now. He's hardly ever home but when he is…' she shrugs. 'He's a lieutenant. Even when he's home, he's a lieutenant. My brother Ben and me, well, we're his men.' She starts pleating her skirt. Her hands are shaking. 'It's awful, really awful, the way he carries on. We're glad when his leave's up and he has to go back.'

'But, Lisa, surely if he's like that your mother won't tell him. She's only trying to scare you.'

'No, she will. You don't know her. You didn't see her face. Oh, I hate her, I hate her.'

I'm shocked. 'But you've always said how close you are, how much she loves you and…'

Lisa's voice is hard. Even her face. I can hardly recognise it. All the softness, the friendliness has gone. It frightens me.

'That was before,' she says. 'She's changed. Anyhow there's something else.' She hesitates. 'Something dreadful. I don't know if I should tell you.' Her voice breaks and she puts her hands over her face. 'Oh, Rhiannon, you have to help me. I haven't got anyone else. You…' She's crying. She doesn't make any noise but all the same I know. 'My mother's got a friend,' she whispers. 'His name is Freddie Kubiak. I thought he was Daddy's friend too. He's been like an uncle, always bringing us presents, flowers for Mother, you know… Ben told me. He told me a while ago but I…I didn't want to believe him.' She fumbles in her pocket for a tissue. I don't say anything. There are little poplar suckers coming up in the grass and I concentrate on them instead.

After a while Lisa goes on. 'Ben's only eleven. He's still at primary school. Oh, Rhiannon have you any idea how embarrassing it is to have your little brother tell you he's found your mother in bed with…' She stops again.

She's crying openly now. Her face is blotched like a child's but her eyes… I don't like what I see in her eyes. I try to say something to comfort her but I can't. There isn't anything.

Then all at once she gives a shaky laugh. 'It's all right, Rhiannon. Don't look like that. It's not so bad.'

For a moment, there is silence. A car goes past. Across the road, a dog begins to bark.

Lisa says, 'Do you think I should blackmail them? Tell her I know about her and Freddie and I can write letters too?'

I shake my head. 'Lisa, I...'

She grabs my hand. Her eyes are wide and frantic. Trapped. The little girl Lisa with her shining hair, the Lisa who seemed to walk in an aura of light, is trapped in those eyes and drowning. 'Tell me, Rhiannon,' she says, her voice strained and unnatural. 'Tell me, Rhiannon-who-always-knows-the-answer, what would you do?' She twists my wrist as she speaks and I know she means to hurt me.

'I wouldn't tell,' I whisper. 'I'd never tell because...'

Lisa leaps to her feet. 'Then you'd be a fool. Oh, I don't know why I bother with you. You're such a baby. You know that, don't you? You live in a world of dreams. You think it's important to be good. You think God cares.'

'I don't believe in God,' I whisper, red-faced, but she isn't listening.

'Can't you understand?' Lisa says, sitting down again. 'If I tell, I'll be safe. She won't dare say anything about Scott and, if she does, well, I can convince Daddy she's lying. And Daddy will get rid of her. Once he finds out about Freddie, he'll come home for good. He won't leave me and Ben with her. She'll have to go and it'll serve her right. She won't be Lieutenant Anderson's wife then. Oh, no. She'll be nobody. That's what she's done to me. All my life. Tried to make me nobody, tried to make me nothing but an extension of herself. Only I'm not. I'm not.'

'Lisa,' I protest. 'Lisa, you can't. You...'

'Shut up, Rhiannon. You ought to approve. It's only fair. Shouldn't the guilty be punished? Don't you believe that, Rhiannon?'

My mouth is so dry, I can hardly speak. 'I...I don't know.' Then suddenly, I find courage. 'There's too much pain in the world. That's what I think. And how will it make you feel better, Lisa, hurting her? I mean, her guilt is hers, let her bear it. As long as you are innocent, you are free.'

'Innocent!' Lisa's lip curls. 'I'm not innocent. I don't even want to be. I want...' She laughs. 'I want power. Tell me, Rhiannon-who-is-so-good, haven't you ever wanted revenge? Haven't you ever wanted to hurt someone?'

I get up clumsily. 'I don't want to talk about it. I'm going back to the classroom to finish my maths assignment.'

Lisa laughs scornfully. 'You're a coward, Rhiannon. You know that, don't you? You're frightened of the truth.'

Lisa is very late the next morning. She slips in during home room and sits down next to me. She looks ill. All the bloom has gone from her skin and her eyes are wide and sort of stretched as if she's seen something she can't forget.

I say, under cover of getting out my books, 'Lisa, I'm sorry about yesterday.'

She nods but that's all. I'm a bit put out. After all, it was her fault. She could at least acknowledge it.

But later, on the way to Physics prac., she slips her arm through mine. 'Something's happened,' she says. 'I'll tell you at lunchtime.' She hesitates a moment and then says in a rush. 'You are my friend, aren't you, Rhiannon? My best friend?'

I know that's not true. I know she's only saying it but it doesn't matter. It's something, an acknowledgement of something, so I say quickly. 'All right.' I'm still hurt, though. I'd rather she said she was sorry. Because she's wrong. Of course she is. I'm not frightened of the truth. I know I'm not.

I never get a chance to tell her, though. I wait for her on the lawn all lunchtime but she doesn't turn up. She doesn't come to Chemistry either or German.

Over the next few days, there are all kinds of rumours. Lisa has been hit by a car and is in hospital. She has run away. She's pregnant and is having a termination. I don't believe any of them. Something bad has happened to her though. I know that. Under the poplar trees I failed her and now…

Then my own life changes. My father finds out about my mother's drinking and, despite my protests, makes arrangements for me to move interstate. I forget Lisa. I don't mean to, but there are so many things to get used to. My grandparents. A new school. Different subjects. I concentrate on fitting in. I want to be like everyone else. It's dangerous to be different.

Only, now the dreams have started. Night after night. They haunt me. And sometimes Lisa is a little girl, frowning as she recites her catechism and sometimes her face is white and strained and the shadows of the poplar trees waver across it.

I have to find her. It's an obsession. Everywhere I go, I expect to see her…the supermarket, the park, the bookshop where I work. I stare into the faces of women in the street and am bewildered when they flinch away. Once, staggering out of bed half-asleep, I think I see her reflection in my mirror. She is smiling, her eyes soft like when she told me I was pretty. My heart leaps. She's all right, then. She's happy. I run to her but the image fades. It's just an illusion. I sigh. The one thing I know for sure is Lisa isn't happy. That's why I'm dreaming about her. She wants me to find her. She needs me.

I pick up the phone book. It's not so long ago. Maybe I can find her address. Maybe I can find her father's name. Lieutenant Kenneth Anderson. And they'd live in a suburb near the school. Brookton. Acacia Park. Clovelly. But none of the Andersons listed can possibly be the right one. I find an F.R. Kubiak, though. Freddie. Surely it would do no harm to check, to ask him… I'm looking for Lisa Anderson… I used to go to school with her a few years ago… I remember her mentioning you, a friend of the family…

I don't phone, though. I try to but it seems too impersonal. I decide to call round instead; it's not too far to walk. I dress with care. My new linen suit. I laugh. Lisa would expect me to wear a long flowing skirt and sandals, my hair all over the place, Alice-in-Wonderland. But I've grown up. Grandma saw to that. My hair is short. I look smart, sophisticated. I smile uneasily at my reflection. Lisa won't recognise me.

I find the house without too much trouble. Number 16. It's just like all the others in the street. Double brick. Tiled roof. A silver birch tree in a carefully manicured lawn. The man who opens the front door is short, almost bald with a round, genial face.

'My name is Rhiannon Carmichael,' I say quickly. 'I went to school with Lisa Anderson. I'm trying to find her. I thought you might…'

He nods and steps back from the door. 'Come in,' he says and, obediently, I follow him.

'Ilse,' he calls. 'Ilse.' He ushers me into an elaborately decorated room and indicates that I should take a seat.

I stare around me. Brocade curtains, a marble mantelpiece dominated by a gold carriage clock, leather lounge suite, a turquoise jardinière of peacock feathers on a mahogany stand… It's all rather overpowering.

'Ilse,' Freddie calls again.

I have never met Lisa's mother but I recognise her immediately when she comes in. She's like Lisa. The same fine, brown hair, the same oval face, smooth and tanned, the same cheekbones…this is Lisa's face grown-up. Even the way she walks. Lisa had that, a careless confidence…

Freddie smiles at her. 'This is a friend of Lisa's. They went to school together. I remember her talking about Rhiannon, don't you, Ilse?'

Ilse barely acknowledges me. There is a packet of cigarettes on an occasional table and she reaches for it. 'Is Lisa expecting you?' she asks, sitting down and lighting a cigarette. Her eyes flick toward me. They are full of mockery.

'No,' I stammer. 'Perhaps I should have rung first but I wasn't sure she'd be here. I…'

Ilse raises a delicately arched eyebrow. 'Where else would she be? A daughter belongs with her mother.'

'Yes, but well…' I look toward Freddie and he comes smoothly to my rescue.

'Things have changed you know, Ilse. Girls leave home at a ridiculously young age now, isn't that so Rhiannon?'

I nod. I feel uncomfortable, almost as if I'm a child again. 'I'm sorry,' I say. 'I shouldn't have just turned up like this. It's probably an inconvenient time too. I…I just wanted to find Lisa.' I look down at my hands in my lap. Even they seem to have undergone a metamorphosis. My nails look ragged, uneven. I force myself to meet Ilse's eyes. 'Lisa and I were…she was my best friend and then, well, she left so suddenly and I had to go away too but now I'm back. I keep thinking about her, remembering…'

Ilse's eyes are cold. 'I don't recall her mentioning you.' She carefully stubs out her cigarette. 'I can't imagine her being friends with you. You're not her type.' She laughs. It is a thin, bitter sound, brittle as glass.

Freddie says, 'Ilse, for heaven's sake…' He goes over to her and puts an arm around her shoulder.

Ilse doesn't look at him, her face goes sullen and she reaches again for her cigarettes.

Freddie turns to me then. 'Rhiannon,' he says. I don't like the way he draws out my name. He makes it sound intimate, as if we have some kind of a relationship. He smiles at me over Ilse's head. 'Rhiannon,' he repeats, 'perhaps you'd like a drink. Tea? Coffee? Fruit juice?'

'No.' My mouth is dry but I shake my head. 'Nothing, thank you.'

Ilse slips off her sandals and crosses one elegant leg over the other. 'Lisa will be home soon. She has a job in the city. One of those new boutiques. What's it called, Freddie? Spangles? Something frivolous like that anyway. Very upmarket of course. Lisa always had impeccable taste.'

'But,' I protest. 'Lisa wanted to be a teacher.' I shake my head. 'She went on and on about it. She…'

Ilse shrugs. 'That was then. She was a child.'

Freddie interrupts us. 'Lisa was ill. That's why she had to leave school. You probably didn't realise. Most people didn't. And then, of course, when she got better, she'd missed so much we thought…'

Ilse doesn't let him finish. 'There's no need to go into that. It's got nothing to do with Rhiannon.'

Her hands are shaking and I watch them fascinated. She's got very white slender hands and I can't help feeling sorry for them. They seem so helpless. Perhaps it's the way she catches hold of them to keep them still.

I swallow. 'Is…is it all right for me to wait for Lisa? I mean, if you'd rather, I could come back or…or maybe I could meet her in town…'

'No, no,' Freddie says, his arm tightening around Ilse. 'Of course you can wait here. Lisa will be delighted to see you.'

Ilse, frowning, throws off his arm. She gets up and comes over to me. 'You're wasting your time,' she says. 'Lisa won't be interested in you. She's got a lot of friends now, girls who know where they're going, girls who…' Then, unexpectedly, her face softens and she reaches forward to touch my cheek. 'Don't you know, child?' she asks gently. 'It's best to let the past go.'

Before I can answer, she turns and, all in a moment, she's gone. Freddie hurries after her. I can hear him calling her name as he follows her down the passageway.

It's very quiet. On the wall, above the chesterfield, there is a portrait of a little girl running across a field of yellow flowers. The sun is behind her. Her hair is a halo of light around her little, laughing face. I want very badly for it to be a picture of Lisa, though I know it could just as easily be one of Ilse.

Freddie comes back. He's affable, apologetic.

I sit down and smooth my skirt over my knees. 'Are you sure it's all right for me to stay,' I ask again.

'Of course.' He lights a cigarette and leans back in his chair. 'You mustn't let Ilse upset you. She…' He pauses; he is choosing his words carefully, his eyes scrutinising my face. 'Things have sometimes been a bit…shall we say…tense between Lisa and her mother. I'm sure you understand. Adolescence. It's never easy, is it? And there was the divorce as well. Naturally that upset Lisa and Ilse – well, Ilse found it impossible to deal with, bringing up the children alone. Their father – he was never at all supportive, only interested in his career. No wonder Ilse turned to me but Lisa… She was so bitter, said such dreadful things… We didn't know she was sick but Ilse blames herself, feels she failed her.' He smiles. 'Ilse tries to put it all behind her. She's very brave, a marvellous woman, but you… well, you've reminded her. Not that it's your fault, of course not, but…'

I can't look at him. I feel the blood rush into my cheeks. 'I shouldn't have come,' I whisper, picking at a broken fingernail.

'Oh, come now, my dear. It's all right.' He reaches over and puts his hand on my arm. 'You know, Rhiannon, my dear, I really think we need a cup of coffee. It won't take long. You wait here and I'll bring it in.' He hesitates a moment. 'I'm sure you were a good friend to Lisa.'

I shake my head. I'm confused. There's something important he hasn't told me, something that he's left out deliberately because… I stare down at my hands. It doesn't matter. Lisa will be here soon. Ilse's right. The past, whatever happened, is over. Lisa and I can begin again.

Freddie and I drink our coffee in silence. Mine is too strong but I don't complain. I stir in several spoonfuls of sugar and make myself drink it. Freddie keeps smiling at me and nodding. I have the peculiar sensation that he can tell what I am thinking. I try to keep my mind blank.

At last he says, 'Tell me, Rhiannon, I've always wondered. What on earth did you girls find to talk about? All day at school together and then in the evenings, the telephone.'

I try to smile. 'It wasn't me. Not on the telephone. My mother…' I put down my cup and start again. 'Lisa and I had lunch together at school. That's all.' I force myself to laugh. My voice sounds high and unnatural. 'We talked about boys, of course. What else do young girls talk about except boys?' Suddenly I have an image of Lisa and myself under the poplar trees, our faces earnest, our hands reaching out to one another and I'm ashamed. I pick up my cup and hold it to my lips. I'm close to tears.

The front gate clangs and Freddie jumps up. I hear his voice at the door. 'Lisa! A wonderful surprise! Rhiannon is here. Your friend from school.'

Against the light, I see a young woman. She walks with an easy grace, her skirt swirls around her bare, brown legs. I run towards her, holding out my hands and laughing. "Lisa, Lisa, I'm so glad I've found you. I…'

Lisa shakes her hair back from her face. It's a gesture I don't remember. She frowns a little, her eyes searching my face. 'Rhiannon?' she says. 'Rhiannon?' Then she shrugs. 'Yes, Rhiannon. Of course.' She ignores my out-stretched hands and sits down in her mother's chair. Slipping off her sandals, she reaches for the packet of cigarettes.

I watch her hands. They are so white and slender… When we were schoolgirls, surely they were different; they faltered, hesitant, they reached out and touched my hair…

I glance over at Freddie. He's pouring Lisa a cup of coffee. I wish he'd leave us alone. Lisa and I…we have nothing to do with him.

'I've been thinking about you such a lot, Lisa, ever since I got home from Melbourne.' I give a little laugh. 'I've even dreamt about you.'

'Really?' Lisa leans back in her chair. 'How extraordinary! I never remember my own dreams.'

'I had to find you. I…' My voice sounds childish, desperate. My cheeks are burning but I can't stop myself. 'I miss you, Lisa,' I whisper. Then I lift my head and look at her.

She is regarding me quite dispassionately. It bothers me. Lisa had such beautiful eyes. Dark brown. Full of warmth. I always envied her them. They looked so startling with her honey-coloured hair. The eyes of the girl in front of me are dark brown too. But they're not the same. Something has gone out of them, something important. It's left them quite empty.

I struggle to my feet, my hand over my mouth. 'I have to go.' I swallow hard. 'Goodbye, Lisa.' I don't look at the girl in front of me. I'm not saying goodbye to her. I don't know her. I'm saying goodbye to my friend Lisa who lived and laughed and danced in her own aura of light. I know she can't hear me but I have to say it anyway.

It's not until the gate closes behind me that I realise I'm crying. It's the first time that I ever remember crying for someone else.

An Egret Flying

We agree to meet at seven o'clock at the roundabout, the one that's got the sculpture of the egret flying from the light tower. Jess and I are almost late because we stop by for Anya first and she's not ready. She's got on her leather skirt and a top she's made out of two of her mother's scarves and she's busy outlining her lips with metallic blue lipstick. Jess raises her eyebrows and mouths 'Ridiculous' at me but I keep my face carefully blank. I've crossed Anya before. It's not something I like thinking about.

When we finally get to the roundabout, Jess is relieved. No one's there except the new girl, Kim. She's sitting on the grass, smiling to herself. She's got this way of doing that as if she knows some secret you don't. Jess frowns. She doesn't like Kim. She goes around the other side of the light tower and leans against one of the boulders there.

Vanessa and Tim are next. They're hand in hand. Vanessa's all flushed and sort of breathless. I smile at her and then turn quickly away. It hurts looking at her. Happiness ought to make people strong. Invincible. Maybe if it's Jess or Anya it does, but with Vanessa it's different. She's suddenly too vulnerable. I bite at my lip and try to work out why.

Damo and Ryan and Gianni get dropped off by Gianni's brother. I'm surprised to see Gianni. He's got a bit of a reputation, nothing serious, just graffiti and stuff but he's never bothered with us before.

Damo glances round at us all. He seems tense, though. Perhaps he's not too sure about Gianni either. 'Where's Finn?' he asks at last. 'Thought he'd be here by now.'

'Perhaps he's not coming,' suggests Kim, bringing up her knees and hugging them. 'Perhaps something came up and he forgot.'

'He wouldn't do that,' says Damo. 'Though last night we…'

I look at him quickly. There's something in his voice. An edge to it. He's quarrelled with Finn again, I think, and my hands clench by themselves and my mouth goes dry. I watch everyone. I have to. I'm so much younger, Jess's little sister. But I don't watch Damo for myself, not entirely. I watch him for Finn as well because Finn's…'special', I whisper, and I'm suddenly very still. Damo knows Finn's special. Or at least he used to. Now…now I'm not so sure. Finn likes Damo too much. More than he should. More than he likes himself and that's, that's…scary, I think and I let my hair fall over my face and start fiddling with the buttons on my blouse.

'Kim's right,' says Anya unexpectedly. 'He's not coming. Let's go.'

Gianni swaggers up to her. 'You make the rules, eh?'

Anya tosses her head. 'So? What's it to you?'

'Nothing. Nothing at all. I just like to know how things are.'

Anya gives an elaborate shrug but she's watching Gianni too and her mouth curls provocatively. 'I make my own rules,' she says. 'And I've had enough of hanging around here. I'm going.' She glances back over her shoulder. 'With or without the rest of you.'

'Wait,' I shout. 'Wait. There's Finn.'

And sure enough, there he is on the other side of the road, mooching along, head down, hands in his pockets. It's like he's lost in some dream of his own, so I dart across and drag at his arm.

'Come on, Finn,' I say. 'You're late. We almost went without you.'

Finn looks at me, dazed. 'Kylie,' he says but then he begins to smile and it's all right and he follows me up onto the roundabout. 'Well,' he says, spreading wide his hands and grinning. 'Well.'

We set off for the beach. It's become a bit of a tradition. First week of summer. A kind of celebration. We don't go to the proper beach, though, the one the tourists use, that's further up the coast. Our beach is different, a bit of a cove, all wild and rocky. No one goes there much except us. That's why we like it.

I start to smell the salt in the air and I'm suddenly excited. My blood stings in my cheeks and I tip my head back so I can feel the wind in my hair. The sky's changing. It's got the hush of evening in it so the blue's gone all soft like it's dreaming. Damo and Ryan lead the way, then Kim. She's singing to herself and moving her hands in front of her face. Finn, stumbling along next to me, watches them, fascinated. They dance and swoop but they're delicate too. I feel my throat begin to ache and I bite down hard on my lip. There are too many feelings inside me. I want to be like Jess and Anya. For just a little while, I want to think only about myself.

At last we're there. It's different, though. We've stayed away too long, I think, and I feel myself shudder. Lonely. It looks lonely and sad too. The sea's grey, dull almost and too calm; it's as if there's a spell on it, on all of it, the rocks, the narrow stretch of sand, the wheeling gulls, the brooding sky. It isn't ready for us.

Ryan gives a sudden whoop and he's off down the overgrown track that leads to the beach and everyone scrambles after him.

I'm last. I'm half inclined to turn back and go home but Damo shouts up to me, 'Come on, Kylie. Hurry up. We're going to get some driftwood for a fire,' so I push my hair out of my eyes and jump down.

It's all right then. We're like little kids, shouting and laughing. Damo and Tim make a circle of stones on the sand and we all dump our bits of driftwood there.

Ryan finds a long piece of seaweed and chases Kim with it. 'The monster. The monster. Beware the sea monster,' he hisses.

Jess and Vanessa creep up behind him. They've found one of those shark eggs. It gleams like a piece of polished, black leather. Jess thrusts it down the back of his neck and then, clutching one another, they dart away again.

I look for Finn. He's by himself at the water's edge. He isn't doing anything, just watching the gulls, so I clamber across the rocks to join him.

'It's good here, isn't it?' I say but he doesn't answer.

He tilts his head back and goes on watching the gulls. 'Flying,' he says. 'Once they're flying, they're different, aren't they? They're free.'

'But flying's what they do. I mean…'

'No. When they're flying, they're themselves. Their true selves. The rest of the time, they…'

'Oh, Finn,' I say shakily. 'What does it matter? Seagulls, they're just seagulls.'

'No. No, they're…' He stops then and smiles at me but there's nothing in his smile for me. It's too sad. It shuts me out, so I swallow and turn my face away.

The sea's a lot darker now; it's starting to get restless too. Over against the cliffs that guard the cove, it sends up spumes of spindrift, white as mermaid's hair. I wish Finn would watch that instead of the seagulls. Maybe its beauty would distract him.

'Look,' says Finn at last. 'Look, Kylie. They've lit the fire. We'd better go back.'

I don't say anything but I let him take my hand and we go back across the rocks together.

The fire makes us a tribe. We huddle around it, feeling its power and hardly daring to look at one another. All at once, a piece of wood explodes into a shower of sparks. The flames leap up, blue and green and turquoise. It's like the wood's got all the colours of the sea imprisoned in it and we watch them, awed. Behind us, the last light runs along the horizon in a line of gold and I shiver and hold my hands out to the fire. We need it now for protection.

Kim starts to sing. Her voice is thin and hauntingly beautiful. I can't make out the words, perhaps they're not even English, but the sound finds its way inside me and aches there. I glance over at Finn but he's looking at Damo. All the baffled longing of Kim's song is in his face and all of the beauty too. Damo recognises it, his lips quiver but then his expression changes. He stares back at Finn, his eyes defiant, and Finn flinches as if he's been hit.

Ryan picks up a stick and pokes at the fire to make more sparks and we watch them drift like falling stars. With a little cry, Vanessa leaps up to catch one. but Tim, laughing, pulls her down again and wraps both his arms around her.

Anya and Gianni get up and wander off toward the rocks. She's got his leather jacket around her shoulders but it doesn't make her look tough like you'd expect. It dwarfs her so she looks suddenly fragile.

I hear Finn sigh and I move closer to him. He's lying on his stomach now; he's got a handful of sand and he's watching it trickle through his fingers. Damo's behind Ryan; his face is in shadow so I can't tell if he's watching Finn or not. Jess starts one of her endless stories and I make a small grimace. Outside the circle of the fire, it's quite dark.

I shudder and tilt my head back so I can watch the stars come out one by one. They're so far away but they're…'Serene', I think, and the word echoes in my mind and almost reassures me. 'I wish…' I whisper but I can't quite put it into words. All at once I don't want to know about people any more. It hurts too much. I want to be like Vanessa all lit up with happiness or my sister Jess or even bright, glittery Anya. The burden of being myself is too much.

Jess's story ends and the fire dies down to a heap of embers. They look like coral flowers. I want to pick one up and hold it in my hands but of course I know I can't.

'We'd better go,' Damo says abruptly.

'No,' whispers Vanessa, still clinging to Tim. 'I don't want to. I feel…'

'Feelings don't matter,' says Damo, his voice unexpectedly harsh.

'I'm cold,' Finn says, as if Damo hasn't spoken. 'It's too early. We should have waited another week.'

Jess gets up and starts brushing sand off her jeans. 'I said that. I said that but none of you would listen. Next time maybe…'

'Hey,' says Ryan. 'Hey, come on. It's been okay.'

'Yes,' says Vanessa. 'It was waiting for us, the beach. Didn't you feel it? All winter. It was glad we came and now…' Her voice trails away when Jess and Ryan laugh at her but it doesn't matter because she laughs too.

We start off across the sand. Ryan gets a torch out of his pocket and it makes a little pinprick of light for us to follow. When we reach the track leading down to the cove, we turn to one another, laughing with relief. Above us there's the streetlight. It's easy now.

Kim's just ahead of me and, as I climb, I watch her skirt swirl around her legs.

'What about Anya and Gianni?' I ask suddenly. 'Shouldn't we have waited for them?' but Kim just shrugs and goes on without answering.

Behind me, the sea whispers and sighs. Vanessa's right. It doesn't want us to leave.

'Kim,' I say again 'Kim.' I want her to slow down so I can catch up with her. I want to ask her about the song she sang and what it meant because…

She doesn't stop, though, not until we reach the top. The others have gone on ahead but she waits for me under the light. 'You worry too much, Kylie,' she says. 'You must learn not to. It doesn't help.'

'But…'

'I have to go,' she says. 'I live around here.'

I'd forgotten that. 'Kim,' I begin again, but she shakes her head at me. Then she smiles and I feel my heart turn over. I don't know why. It's her smile, I think confused, it's so gentle and yet…

'Poor little Kylie,' she says, and she reaches out her hand and touches my cheek with the tips of her fingers. Then she's gone.

I stand there a moment, staring after her. Frowning, I put my hand up to the place she's touched. I don't understand her but I can still feel the flutter of her fingers against my cheek. A butterfly, I think, it was like a butterfly's wings and yet…and yet…

When we get to the roundabout, Damo and Ryan insist on walking home with us.

'You coming too?' Ryan asks Finn, but he shakes his head, so we leave him there by himself.

He goes over to the light tower and leans against it, looking up at the egret flying. As soon as we've crossed the road, I glance back at him. He's standing very still, his arms stretched out to the egret, his head tilted back. The streetlight makes a silhouette of him except for the haze that's his hair. He's part of the sculpture, I think, part of it and…

Damo puts his arm around me and pulls me close; he's got his other arm around Jess. Ryan's on the other side of her. I laugh. All at once, I feel better. Kim's right. I worry too much. Next time, next time when we go, when it's properly summer, it'll be better. Damo and Finn will have sorted things out. It'll be like last year, all of us friends together…

In the morning when Jess and I wake up, the house is very quiet. Mum's left us a note on the refrigerator. 'Gone shopping. Will be back in time for lunch. M.' I hand it to Jess and pour us both a glass of orange juice. As soon as I've finished mine, I race her to the shower.

I'm towelling myself dry when I hear the phone ring. Jess'll be glad, I think, reaching for my T-shirt; she always makes a fuss if I get to the phone before her. I pull my T-shirt over my head and shake my hair free. Then Jess starts to scream. For a moment, I can't do anything. I watch my hands fall to my sides and I stare at them, confused. It's like they don't belong to me. But the screaming goes on and on until at last it jerks me out of myself. I have to make it stop. Without bothering about my jeans, I wrench open the bathroom door and run into the kitchen.

Jess is by the bench. She's dropped the phone on the floor and she's cowering away from it, the knuckles of one hand jammed in her mouth.

'Jess,' I whisper urgently. 'Jess, what is it?'

'Damo's father. It was Damo's father. He...' Her eyes, wide and bewildered, seek mine. 'He said....he said Finn... He said Finn shot himself. Last night, he shot himself last night and...'

I can't move. Jess runs at me and grabs me. She's sobbing now, choking with it and I feel my arms go around her and I'm holding her but it can't be me because I'm, I'm not there. I'm with Finn. We're standing by the light tower and I'm shouting, 'Why? Tell me why?' but Finn's not listening. He's watching the egret flying. He's crying out to it, he's got his head tilted back and he's smiling...

I can't bear it. All at once, I push Jess away and run into my room and slam the door. I lean against it, panting, and then I let myself slide down and rest my head against my knees.

An egret. An egret flying. I say the words over and over in my mind, it's like if I say them long enough, they'll mean something, something different. And in the end they almost do. I feel something break inside me and I begin to sob. I sob for Finn and Damo and the rest of us. Most of all I sob for the aching, throat-catching beauty of the egret caught forever in a moment of flight.

Hounds of the Hunter

Damian is at the gate again, waiting. Sarah bites down hard on her lip and turns her head away so she doesn't have to look at him.

'You're late,' he says. 'I told you last time. I don't like hanging about.'

Sarah doesn't say anything. There's no point. When they reach the bridge, he grabs her arm and twists it up behind her back. 'That's to warn you,' he says, panting. 'Don't keep me waiting tomorrow.'

Sarah makes a little soundless gasp. It's enough, though.

Damian relaxes and lets go of her. 'All right. Now you know.' He pulls her further under the bridge.

No one can see them there. It's all tangled shadows and empty beer bottles and on the far side, the river itself, a dark thread almost choked with reeds and blackberries.

Sarah grits her teeth. She knows what Damian's going to do and she hates it but she lets him. She has to. The blackberries are in flower, just one or two, little white flowers like stars. Sarah shuts her eyes and the flowers are there inside her mind, she is holding a spray of them in her hand, their little tender stamens are tipped with gold. For a moment it's as if the things Damian is doing aren't happening to her. They're happening to someone else, some other girl who probably likes it. Sarah feels sorry for her. She looks a real loser, the girl with Damian. She's stupid too. Otherwise she wouldn't just lie there… she'd do something, she'd…Sarah shakes her head and opens her eyes.

Suddenly she starts. It's like waking up. Damian is speaking to her. His voice is different. It's so low it's almost a whisper.

He puts out a hand and touches the curve of her cheek. 'You've got nice eyes,' he says. 'Sort of like a fawn. I…' He stops. He looks surprised. Then, almost immediately, his mask is back. His voice deepens. 'I was telling me mate Simmo about you. He wants to come with us tomorrow. He reckons I owe him one and so…'

'No. No.' Sarah shrinks back. Her eyes, her fawn's eyes, are so wide she can feel the skin around them stretching, stretching… 'No. Please. Please don't make me. I…'

Damian straightens up. He swaggers a bit. 'Well,' he says. 'Well, I haven't decided yet. Told him I'd let him know.'

Sarah can't look at him. Her hands are trembling. She pulls down her skirt and then, to hide her face, she bends over and carefully reties one of her shoes.

Damian picks up his school bag and shoulders it. 'Gotta go.' Without a backward glance, he's up on the bank and running along the path to the bus stop.

Sarah hears him begin to whistle. She leans back against the concrete pylon. She feels suddenly too tired to move. She puts her head down on her drawn-up knees and closes her eyes. Her hair falls forward over her face. She feels safe behind it. She thinks about the fawn Damian saw in her eyes. She is standing watching it. A little tender thing stepping delicately toward her through the bleached grass. It pauses a moment, irresolute, its nostrils quivering. It is so innocent. But the hounds are out. She can hear them in the distance. They are baying for its blood. Sarah shudders. The fawn doesn't know. It curls itself up in the grass and goes to sleep.

Sarah wants to save the fawn. And Damian. Damian wants to save it too. Sarah can see it in his face. His mouth is trembling. But his hands, his hands, they twist together and all at once the softness goes out of his face. He is helpless too.

'Victims,' whispers Sarah. Her mouth is dry. She wets her lips with her tongue. 'We are victims. Hunter and hunted. All victims.'

The baying of the hounds is louder than ever. They have almost reached the fawn. Sarah can't bear to watch. She opens her eyes.

The shadows under the bridge have darkened. She can no longer see the fawn or the hounds. Sighing, she reaches for her bag and gets up. It's time to go home.

Marigold Flower

Melissa stands by the table facing her mother. Her hands, white-knuckled, grip the back of a chair. 'I have to,' she whispers. 'You've got to understand, Mum. I have to.'

Her mother says slowly, 'Oh, Lissie. If…if you had the baby, then, then I'd look after it. I'd look after it till you were ready.' She lifts her head and looks into Melissa's eyes. 'As, as soon as you asked, I'd give it back to you. I promise. I'd give it back.'

Melissa winces. She hears the pain in her mother's voice and her mother's eyes, so wide, pleading, her mother's eyes, so young – how can her mother, forty-two with five children, have eyes younger than her own?

She flings back her hair. 'I can't. I can't.' Her voice rises and almost breaks. 'I want it out of me. I can't bear to think of it in there, growing. Every day growing and… I have to… I want it, I want it, gone.'

'All right, then. It's all right. I understand. Truly, Melissa, I understand.'

'And…and you don't blame me. You…you won't hate me because I…'

'Of course not. How could I? You're my child. Whatever you do, you're my child.'

Melissa lets her hair fall over her face. She's done that ever since she was a child. She has to shield herself from her mother. 'Thursday. They've given me an appointment for Thursday. It doesn't take long. I don't even have to stay in overnight.'

Her mother takes a step or two towards her. 'Do you want me to come with you? I mean, you can't go alone and…'

'No. Andrew said he'd come. But,' Melissa's voice hardens and she clenches her fists. 'I don't want him there. He…he doesn't really care. It's, it's like it's nothing to do with him. And…' She stops suddenly. Her eyes, bewildered, seek her mother's.

'You… Oh, Melissa, you can't go alone. I'll come. I'll get Mrs Stevens to mind Ruthie and…'

'No. I don't want you to come. I know how you feel. You couldn't bear it. Honestly.' Melissa's lips quiver. All at once she can see her mother in her mind, years ago when they were all children, her mother, wet-faced, bending over a little dead bird… She straightens up. She can't have the baby to save her mother pain but she can, she can do this. 'Amy said she'd come. Caro's working but Amy isn't. She'll be there. You'd like them, Mum, Amy and Caro. They're… I've never had friends like them before. They've got rules. House rules. We all make them up because otherwise, well, it'd be like when I was sharing that place with Kate. Horrible. Nothing got done and then the bills –'

There's a little silence. Her mother turns to the steaming kettle. 'Tea, Melissa? Or coffee? Or I could do you soup, one of those instant ones you used to like. I've got some in the cupboard…'

Melissa shakes her head. 'I've got to be going, Mum. I'm working tonight. The Noodle Bar. I've got to get the three-thirty train. But…but I wanted to tell you. I wanted to tell you myself because….' She wants to say more. She wants to say she's sorry for all the trouble she's caused her mother, running away, the drugs, the…the anger but the words jam in her throat and she can't get them out. She takes a shuddering breath. 'I'll ring you afterwards. I promise. Thursday night. And…and you won't be upset about it, will you? The baby, I mean. It…it isn't really a baby. Not yet. They said…'

Her mother's head jerks up. Her eyes are suddenly very dark. 'It is a baby, Melissa. Don't pretend otherwise. It's a baby all right.' Then her voice softens. 'But I do understand. Really. I know you can't look after a baby. Not yet. Not the way things are with you. And it's brave of you, yes, brave of you, to recognise it and…'

Melissa concentrates on sliding her fingers up and down the back of the chair. 'I have to go,' she says, but she makes no move toward her backpack.

Her mother, pouring hot water into a mug, says. 'You will ring, Lissie… I won't be able to help worrying and…' She hesitates and then says all in a rush, 'And if you change your mind and decide to keep it…'

'Oh, Mum.' Melissa grabs her bag then. She can't bear the hope in her mother's voice. She isn't going to change her mind and her mother… She's at the door but she turns back. 'I'll ring you. I'll ring you tomorrow and then, then on Thursday. Oh, Mum, Mum, I can't do anything else. I can't.' She wrenches open the door. She's crying. Her tears sting her cheeks. She's suddenly angry. Herself. Her mother. The baby. She's angry with them all and it hurts, this kind of anger, and once, once anger was exhilarating, it was power, making people do what she wanted and now...now...

It's raining. She pauses at the gate. Spring rain. Grey. On the road in front of her there's a marigold flower. Just one. Someone, a child perhaps, has flung a marigold flower onto the road. She stares at it, frowning. Once, last year, last year when she was still at school, she'd have darted out and rescued it. But she can't stop now. If she misses the train, she'll be late for work.

Blood on the Snow

The day after the quarrel, Mia comes home late from the library. Mum's already in the kitchen preparing tea, salad and cold meat and a casserole of scalloped potatoes. Felicity's making a performance out of setting the table. Mia watches her sister for a moment. Ingratiating, she thinks, Felicity is ingratiating herself with Mum again. It's a good word. Condescending and yet elegant. Mia says it over to herself and almost smiles.

Mum looks up. 'Oh, there you are, dear. We were beginning to wonder. We're having tea early. It's our night to visit Grandpa.'

Mia nods. Ever since his fall last month, Grandpa's been in a convalescent home. They take it in turns with Auntie Jean and Uncle Richard and Second Cousin Rosemary to visit him. Mia picks up her bag.

'Just a minute,' says Mum, putting down her knife. 'I met Sylvia Worthington at the supermarket this afternoon. She was very upset. It was embarrassing. It seems there's some sort of trouble between you and Amy.'

Before Mia can answer, Felicity starts. 'Amy was crying at school at lunchtime. I saw her in the girls' toilets. She said you won't speak to her. She said you've made it so Rachel and Charlene won't speak to her either.'

'That's disgraceful, Mia. You know how I feel about that sort of behaviour.' Mum's cheeks begin to redden and she pauses for a moment. 'I told Sylvia we'd take Amy with us this evening. She's always been very fond of Grandpa. And it'll give you a chance to apologise to her without your school friends gawking round. I suppose that's what this is all about. Those new girls you've made friends with. Really, Mia, I did expect something better from you.'

Mia puts her bag down again. She wipes her hands on the back of her jeans. 'I'm not apologising to Amy,' she says. 'I haven't done anything wrong.' She takes a deep breath. 'I won't be going to see Grandpa either. Not if, not if Amy's going.'

There's a sudden silence. Mum's mouth tightens. She picks up her knife and begins slicing the corned beef. 'I see. Well, it's up to you, of course. But I'm disappointed in you. And I'm sure Grandpa will be too. He thinks the world of Amy.'

Words tumble around in Mia's mind. She can see the shape of them but she can't quite catch hold of them. There's no point in trying to explain, but she still needs the words for herself. To repeat in her mind. It's her only defence. Except…except… Perhaps it's best if her mind's blank. That way, her face won't give anything away. She eats her tea in silence. After she's helped Felicity stack the dishwasher, she takes her bag to her room. She's safe there. She puts her books on her desk and feels her self come back. Her real self. She smiles. Her history book's on the top of the pile. Her fingers trace the title. *Europe…a history*. In a sudden rush of tenderness, she picks it up and holds it against her chest.

'I will do maths and science first,' she decides. 'Then history.' She gives a little laugh. It's like making an appointment. They're doing Napoleon in history. 'About an hour,' she says. 'I'll be ready to meet you in an hour.' She can see him in her mind, Napoleon on a white horse, riding ahead of his troops. She smiles at him but he doesn't acknowledge her. She doesn't expect him to. All his energy is concentrated on his men. She is glad of that. Napoleon is leading them into battle. To victory. Even for a great man like Napoleon, victory does not come easily.

Neither her mother nor Felicity comes to say goodbye. Mia pretends she doesn't care. Her mouth trembles a little though when she hears the car start up and she has to bite down hard on her lip to distract herself. She will not think about it. She will not think about them stopping at the Worthingtons' and Amy getting into the car, Amy in her best dress, all smiles and curls and bubbling charm. Her mother, her sister, her grandfather all treating Amy as if she were some kind of princess, as if she were special, as if she were their daughter, their sister, their grandchild… It isn't fair. For years, Amy has done this, has usurped her place and no one has noticed. And…and…it isn't as if Amy has ever shared anything of her life. Amy's got a father, Dr Worthington; she's never shared him with Mia and she should have because Mia hasn't got a father – he left them when she was a baby, he didn't even wait to see if Mia was worth staying for…

Mia grips her history book with both hands. She takes a deep breath. It's all right. It's all right. It doesn't matter. It doesn't matter. Felicity, Mum, Grandpa, Amy. I am going to Austerlitz with Napoleon and nothing can defeat us. Nothing can defeat us because, because what does it say… 'the strength of his will appears most of all in his ability to master himself'. It's like a message. As if Napoleon, on his white charger, has turned and smiled at her. She can master herself. She can hide how she feels. She's been doing it for years…

Mum and Felicity are late coming home. Mia's already in bed.

Mum pauses at her doorway to say goodnight. 'It's a pity you didn't come,' she says. 'We went for pizza afterwards. The girls really enjoyed themselves. You're being very silly, carrying on like this.'

Mia doesn't answer and after a while Mum makes a little impatient noise and goes away. Mia smiles. She's proud of herself. She's like Napoleon. She can master herself.

Amy comes up to her the next day. She's got her hair done a different way, all piled up on the top of her head in a froth of curls. 'Your grandfather was disappointed you didn't come last night,' she says. 'I told him you had too much homework. I don't think he believed me, though. I think he thought you didn't want to see him.'

Mia's lips quiver but she concentrates on getting her books out of her locker. She slams it shut and carefully, one by one, puts her books in her backpack.

'Your mum has invited me again,' says Amy. 'Friday. I hope you come this time. There were some really cute boys at the pizza place. When your mum was ordering, one of them turned around and winked at me.'

Mia picks up her bag. She's remembered something. She's remembered Moscow. The soldiers following Napoleon stumble in the snow. On the long march, their boots have worn out and now their feet are bleeding. They've tied them up with rags but there's blood on the snow. In the waning afternoon light, she can see the blood on the snow but the soldiers, stumbling, keep on going. They have committed themselves to a cause and he rides ahead of them, lonely, valiant, but still, oh always, their leader.

Mia shoulders her bag. She doesn't even glance at Amy. Loyalty, she thinks. My mother and my sister, they don't know anything about loyalty.

They've betrayed me. They want Amy instead of me. But it's all right. It's all right. They can't make me betray myself. Oh, never that. I don't want to be friends with Amy any more. I don't like her. I don't think I ever have. And…and I'm thirteen. It's time I decided things for myself. I'm stumbling in the snow after Napoleon. I know, I know that after Moscow comes Waterloo but I don't care. I don't care. I won't desert him. I will be loyal to Napoleon and to myself…

Mia lifts her chin. She's heard the sound of the bugle. She walks past Amy and down the corridor. The music swells inside her till it's louder than the sound of her own heart.

from *Tiger! Tiger!*

The Tiger

Tiger, tiger, burning bright
In the forests of the night,
What immortal hand or eye
Could frame thy fearful symmetry?

In what distant deeps or skies
Burnt the fire of thine eyes?
On what wings dare he aspire?
What the hand dare seize the fire?

And what shoulder and what art
Could twist the sinews of thy heart?
And when thy heart began to beat,
What dread hand and what dread feet?

What the hammer? what the chain?
In what furnace was thy brain?
What the anvil? What dread grasp
Dare its deadly terrors clasp?

When the stars threw down their spears,
And water'd heaven with their tears,
Did He smile His work to see?
Did He who made the lamb make thee?

Tiger, Tiger burning bright
In the forests of the night
What immortal hand or eye
Dare frame thy fearful symmetry?

William Blake 1757–1827

Tiger

It's over. The tiger has retreated again to the long grass to sleep.

Soon Mum and Amy will be back from the shops. They don't know about the tiger, otherwise they wouldn't have left me with him.

I go over to the window and put my hand against the cool glass. Outside, the garden is full of sunshine. It looks safe, safer than in here where he…

We learnt about tigers at school. Last year. The year before. I'm not sure. I remember shuddering, though. I remember shuddering when the teacher showed us the pictures. 'Predator,' she said. 'The tiger is a predator, an alpha predator.' There were antelope in one of the pictures…antelope running… I close my eyes to make them go away.

Sighing, I turn away from the window and go out of my room and across the passage into the bathroom to wash my face and hands. I comb my hair and tie it back Then I go outside to sit on the veranda steps. I make a picture of myself in my mind, Phoebe Taylor with her hands folded primly in her lap and her hair spread out in a fan across her shoulders, good little Phoebe Taylor who has finished all her homework and is waiting now for her mother to come back from the shops.

I'm not sure what she'd do if she knew the truth.

****

I stand at the bathroom door, watching Mum give Amy her bath. Amy squints up her eyes and slaps at the water with both her hands.

'Careful,' warns Mum. 'Careful. You'll splash your sister.'

I hold myself very still. She's always saying that but it isn't true.

'How can Amy be my sister?' I ask. 'We haven't got the same father.'

'Oh, Phoebe, that doesn't matter. You know it doesn't. We're still a family. You, me, Amy and Steve.'

I don't say anything. I can't. The feelings inside me are too mixed up. Steve isn't my father. I watch my fingers slide up and down the door frame. Amy isn't my sister, not my proper sister, not like the ones you read about in books where they hold hands and go to school together and share things. She can't ever be that kind of sister because Steve's her father and he…he…

'Mum…' I say but then I stop. I can't tell her. She's changed too much. Before, before when it was just her and me, she was different. She made up things. Not bad things. Pretending. 'Flamingoes,' I whisper, remembering. 'The flamingoes in the park.' And in the winter, when it was so cold we had to wrap ourselves in blankets, we'd listen to the polar bears snuffling outside the back door.

Steve didn't like it. 'You're filling her head full of nonsense, Kerry,' he said, so after a while she stopped. Everything stopped. The paper flowers we used to make, the candles, the beads, the little families of clay echidnas. Mum cut her hair and stopped going to the markets. She got a proper job instead.

'Mum,' I say suddenly. 'Mum, where is my father? Why doesn't he come and see me?'

'He…' she begins but then her face closes up and she turns back to Amy. 'I don't know.'

'I'd like to see him,' I whisper but she pretends not to hear. It's like that now. Everything's something it's not. Steve. My mother. Even me.

***

Between the house and the garage there's a wild bit, all overgrown with ivy. I like it there. It's The Secret Place.

Mum comes out to hang the washing on the line. Amy's pink overalls, her little shirts, my checked school dress, my jeans, my dark blue windcheater. My clothes make Amy's look like dolls'.

Mum picks up the empty basket and goes over to the fence to talk to Mrs Anderson. '…it's a real worry for us. Phoebe's so jealous of the baby. It's been going on ever since Amy was born. You'd think by now she'd have got over it…'

I hunch up my knees and rest my cheek on them. Through the fall of my hair I watch the ivy leaves. Heart-shaped, they quiver in the light. The old leaves are dull and tired but the little new ones glow green and tender as if they've just been hatched.

My mother's still talking. 'He's marvellous with her, simply marvellous, a real father. Always bringing her home little things he thinks she'll like, coloured pens, posters for her room, computer paper from his work. Most of the time she won't even look at them…'

I grab a spray of ivy and start to tear off all its leaves but it doesn't make me feel better.

***

Antelope are prey. I found out about them in a book during Library. They're red-brown with slender legs and big wondering eyes. Some of them have horns all twisted into spirals but it doesn't make any difference. They can't protect themselves. That's the thing. The prey belong to the predator. He can do whatever he wants to them.

***

I go to school the long way. I'm meant to stop off and call for Jenny but I don't. I don't want to. My friends. Jenny. Bethany. Sarah-Louise. I don't want to talk to any of them.

At recess, though, Jenny grabs me by the arm. 'What's going on, Phoebe?' she demands. 'Where were you? I waited and waited. You made me late.'

I pull away from her but Bethany's there in front of me. Her eyes are mean. It surprises me. I thought she liked me.

'You ought to at least answer,' she says, tossing her head. 'It's rude not to.'

'Yeah.'

I glance desperately from one to the other. Their faces have changed. Jenny. Bethany. Sarah-Louise. It's like I don't know them. It's like I've never seen them before.

My mouth's gone dry. 'I…' I begin but it's too late

'Come on,' says Bethany. 'Leave her alone. She's in one of her moods. Let's go and shoot goals with Samantha Ellis.'

81

Sarah-Louise hesitates a moment. 'Hey, wait up, don't you think…?' but when the other two don't answer, she turns and runs after them.

I go over and sit on the bench outside the sickroom. No one ever sits there except Gretta Carson, whom no one likes.

***

I walk slowly home from school. The leaves are beginning to fall, red and orange and butter-yellow. They drift past me like stars. I stand very still and put out my hand to catch one. It quivers in the palm of my hand as if it's still alive. It makes me sad. I trace around it carefully with one finger and then I let it go again.

I go back to looking at gardens. It's the best thing about walking home by myself. I try to make the things I see into pictures. Blue flowers spilling out of a concrete urn. Birds. A little excited dog. A tree with dark pink flowers that look like they're made of paper. I stop to stare at them and then I shut my eyes quickly to see if I can still see them. That's the test. If I can see them with my eyes closed, they'll be inside me forever. Even at night, even when he comes, they'll still be there and I can…I can…

All at once I start to shudder. The tiger's image is too powerful. It blocks out everything else.

'Lily. Lily.'

I whirl round, startled. Just up from me there's an old lady leaning on a wooden gate. She's smiling and calling out to me. 'Lily, I've been waiting for you. I've made us some lemonade…'

'I…I think you've made a mistake. My name's Phoebe and I…'

'Oh, Lily.' She puts both her hands up to her mouth and giggles. 'The games you play. Whatever would Mother say? My own sister. Phoebe! Phoebe indeed!' She opens the gate. 'Come on in. I've made the lemonade just the way you like it with plenty of sugar.'

I'm not sure what to do. I know what my mother would say…but… but…a long time ago when my mother was different, when we were at the markets…she'd smile at everyone… A man with dreadlocks and dirty, calloused hands, she let him have a whole family of echidnas for free because he said he liked them. I remember him picking them up, 'They fit my hands,' he said and my mother smiled… She doesn't smile like that now. Her eyes have changed…but…but…I lift my head. The old lady's smile…it's like hers used to be…welcoming…

'All right.' I say and follow her up the path and onto the veranda.

She settles me in an old cane chair and hands me a beaker of lemonade. 'I was hoping you'd come today,' she says, arranging herself carefully in her own chair. 'I need your advice.'

'I don't think I…'

'It's the tulips.'

'Tulips…?'

'The spring bulb catalogue came this morning and I can't make up my mind. I thought I'd plant tulips all around the bird bath but I don't know which to order, the pink or the yellow.'

'But aren't tulips red. I thought…'

She stares at me a moment and then, suddenly, she laughs and claps her hands. 'You're right, Lily. Of course. Red. The grey stone and then when the forget-me-nots come out, a haze of blue and the tulips like red-painted soldiers. Oh, Lily, you are clever.'

I don't know what to say so I smile and take another sip of lemonade. I like what she's said, though. She's like me. She makes things into pictures.

After a while I put my empty glass on the little table between us and pick up my backpack. 'I'd better go. My mother will be wondering where I am.'

'I'll see you to the gate.' At the gate, though, she hesitates. I watch her hands flutter over the latch as she opens it. 'You'll come back won't you?' she says. 'Now you know I'm here, waiting, you'll come back, won't you?'

Her eyes seek for mine and before I can stop myself, I say, 'Yes. Yes, I will.' I take a deep breath and lift my chin. 'If I'm Lily,' I say carefully, 'you've got to have a name too. It's no good if you don't have a name too.'

'Beatie. My name's Beatie. Beatrice, it's short for Beatrice.'

'Beatie,' I repeat. 'Beatie and Lily.' I like the sound of it, the sound of our names together. 'See you tomorrow then.' I turn and start running. Even that feels good. I haven't run anywhere for a long time.

***

Easter. We have to go to church. He insists. Amy sits on Mum's lap holding her new Flopsybunny against her cheek. Ever since she got it this morning, she won't let go of it. Her curls are all fluffed out around her face and when she smiles you can see her dimples. I turn my head quickly away.

The priest tells about Mary Magdalene and the empty tomb and then the choir gets up to sing but I stop listening. I think about Jesus dying instead. Only, now when I think about him, he doesn't seem like a man nailed to a cross at all but an antelope or a gazelle or maybe a frightened, half-grown fawn. They're hunting him down, all of them. I feel myself shudder. God. God's doing it too because he's letting it happen even though Jesus is his son and he's meant to look after him.

I stare down at the floor where the light from the stained glass windows is making coloured patterns. Red. Blue. Green. The colours look alive but of course they're not.

***

Beatie's garden is full of butterflies. We sit on the veranda and watch them.

'There aren't any butterflies where I live,' I say slowly. 'Only birds and cats.' My hand flutters against my throat but I make my voice go on as if I am talking about something ordinary. 'Mrs Anderson's cat is always coming into our garden.'

Beatie's face puckers in consternation. 'Don't you like cats any more, Lily? You used to. Remember the wild kittens in the hay in the feed-shed? Little scraps of things they were, so fierce, hissing and spitting, but you didn't care. You'd put your hand right in and pick one up.'

I lift my head. 'Cats are predators,' I say. 'They kill things.'

'Of course. Nothing like a good mouser.'

'No,' I whisper. 'No. It's more than that. If they didn't like it so much then…' I take a deep breath. 'They never kill anything straight away. They always have to play with it first.'

'Oh, Lily. It's not like that. They do what they have to.'

She's wrong. She doesn't know. I've watched Mrs Anderson's cat. It's cruel. Even when it's playing with a leaf, you can tell it's wishing it was a bird or a mouse.

84

Beatie leans over and takes my hand. 'Look at the butterflies in the lavender, Lily.' she says. 'White butterflies among the purple lavender.'

I know what she's doing. She's making a picture in her mind for afterwards. I pull my hand away. 'I have to go,' I say, jumping up and grabbing my backpack.

Pictures aren't any good. They don't work. The things they block out always come back. I wrench open Beatie's gate and start to run. Running helps. I do it a lot now, one street after another, until it's almost dark. It makes my mind go blank and keeps everything else out..

***

When he's the tiger, he doesn't say anything. I don't either. It's better like that. I shut my eyes and turn my face to the wall. The sun's setting behind the trees and the antelope…the little antelope comes down to the water to drink. She's by herself. The rest of them stay in the trees. They don't even know she's gone…

He lets go of me suddenly. 'Tomorrow,' he says. 'Tomorrow, Phoebe, I'm going to get you something special.'

'I don't want…'

'Yes. Yes, you do. Wait. Wait till you see what I get you.' His voice sounds wrong. As if, now he's the tiger, talking hurts. 'I'm going to get you a rose bush,' he whispers. 'A little miniature rose bush. I saw one at the market today and I thought…' He puts his hand out and touches my cheek.

I'm frightened then. I'm frightened because when he touches my cheek it feels different. It feels like he cares about me.

My mother doesn't. She only cares about Amy. When she looks at me, she doesn't even see me. She used to but now she doesn't.

***

Saturday's my birthday. I'll be twelve then. I don't feel twelve. I feel… I don't know what I feel.

I stare at my face in the mirror. It's a nothing sort of face. Eyes. Nose. Mouth. They're all there in the right places but that's it. They don't mean anything. I look like a rag doll. I grab hold of my hair and hold it on top of my head but it doesn't change anything. 'Stupid,' I whisper. 'A stupid rag doll.'

Mum calls me from the kitchen. 'Phoebe, come here a minute. We haven't talked about your party.'

I turn the mirror to the wall and go down the passage to join her.

'I don't want a party,' I say. 'I haven't got anyone to invite.'

'Oh, don't be silly. What about Jenny? What about Bethany and Sarah-Louise?'

'They're not my friends.'

'Oh, Phoebe.' She sets the iron on its stand and carefully hangs Steve's shirt over the back of a chair. 'Perhaps I could ring Jenny's mother. If you're having problems…'

'No,' I shout. 'No. I just don't like Jenny any more. Or Bethany. Or Sarah-Louise. They're…' I stop. I can hardly breathe but I make myself go on. 'Beatie,' I whisper. 'I've got a new friend, Beatie, but she's busy on Saturdays so she wouldn't be able to come.'

My mother's still frowning. She reaches into the clothes basket and shakes out one of Amy's dresses. 'Perhaps a picnic then, just you and me and Amy and Steve. We could go down by the river. You'd like that, wouldn't you, a family picnic?'

I don't answer. We're not a family. We can't be. She and Steve and Amy are a family but I'm not.

I go back to my room and get my painting things out of my desk drawer. It's a new thing. Not pictures. I don't want to do pictures. I sit cross-legged on the floor and tear a page out of the sketch pad I've got for school. Colours. That's what I like. Seeing what happens with colours. I mix purple and black together and swirl them across the paper with my fingers. 'A serpent,' I whisper, full of wonder, and then my heart starts to beat very fast because a serpent's powerful and sinister too so it could… it could… 'Devour,' I say aloud and, before I can stop myself, I grab up the tube of crimson paint and squeeze it all out until the page is covered with a pool of blood.

***

It's Sunday afternoon. I'm home by myself. They're at the zoo with Amy. I wouldn't go with them. I'm too old for the zoo. I know too much. The animals don't like it there. Last time I went I felt… I felt…

I sit by the window and look at the sky. It's full of light. I press my hands hard against the glass. The light is so beautiful.

I get up slowly and go over to my desk. I pick up one by one my little tubes of paint. Crimson. Orange. Blue. Yellow. Green. White. Sighing, I put them down again. No matter how I mix them, I can't paint light. No one can.

***

I help Beatie plant the tulip bulbs around the bird-bath.

'There,' she says, dusting her hands together when we've finished. 'Nothing to do now but wait for spring.'

I look doubtfully at the bare, churned earth. Even when I shut my eyes I can't see the flowers.

Beatie can, though. 'Magic,' she whispers. 'I always think it's magic, things growing.' She shakes her head as if to change the pictures inside her mind and reaches out to touch my hair. 'Such pretty hair, Lily. Do you remember how Mother used to put it up in rags on Saturday nights so she could make it into ringlets for church on Sundays? She never had to with mine, it curled by itself, but yours was such a pretty colour. Candied honey, Father said, just the colour of candied honey.'

I don't say anything. I'm never sure if she really believes I'm Lily. Sometimes I think it's just a game and I get frightened. If…if she finds out I'm not Lily, if I say anything to spoil it, then…then…

'Come along,' says Beatie, suddenly brisk. 'You put the watering can and trowel away in the shed and I'll go and get our drinks. Hot cocoa, this afternoon, I thought, with some of my ginger snap biscuits.'

We sit on the veranda together. I lean back in my chair and turn my mug around in my hands to warm them.

'Look,' says Beatie, pointing. 'Look over there in the rose bushes. Thornbills.'

I turn my head. Four, five, but all in a moment they're darted away and there's nothing left but a trembling of the leaves.

'I've got some birds,' I say slowly. 'My stepfather gave them to me for my birthday. They're in a cage in my room, a blue wooden cage…' I stop. I'm not sure about my birds. A cage…their wings…their little beating wings…

Beatie smiles and turns toward me. 'Canaries? Grandfather had canaries.'

I shake my head. 'No. He said they were finches. Zebra finches.' I put my mug down and busy myself with straightening the hem of my school skirt. 'They're pretty. They've got stripes and orange beaks and they're never still. They hop from one perch to the other and…' I lift my head to look at her. 'I'm not sure they're happy, though. I'm not sure they can be happy. My room…my room isn't a happy place.'

Beatie doesn't say anything but her eyes meet mine and it's as if she knows, as if, though I've never said anything, she knows about him and what he does and the darkness that's growing inside me, choking me.

'We'll have to look in the garden for thistles,' she says after a while. 'Grandfather's canaries liked thistles. Maybe finches like them too.'

I don't say anything. I can't. But she's made it all right. She's made it all right for me to keep my birds.

***

I go to the library after school to get a book about finches. I have to ask the librarian for help but she doesn't seem to mind. There are different kinds. Red-browed. Double-barred. Gouldian. I hold the book up in front of my finches so they can see the pictures. 'It says you come from all over Australia,' I say and I read them 'I love a sunburnt country' out of my school poetry book to help them remember. They turn their heads to the side and watch me out of their round, black eyes.

'Oh,' I whisper. 'Oh,' and I'm suddenly frightened because I love them and I don't want to.

***

The tiger's got gold eyes. I watch the little antelope come down to the water-hole and I see them. I see them watching her. She lifts her narrow

88

head and the water drips from her muzzle. It's gold too. Everything, sky, ground, the stunted trees, everything's black or gold so she doesn't see, she can't see. The tiger stretches himself in the long grass and the shadows that slide over him are black and gold too.

'Phoebe.'

Startled, I open my eyes.

Steve's turned on my bedside lamp. The shadows across his face make him look different. Sad. 'Phoebe,' he says again. 'I don't want to do this. You know I don't… You make me,' he whispers. 'You know you do.'

'No.' I feel my lips move…the antelope, the little antelope…but I know I haven't said anything.

He brings his hand up and touches my face. 'I love you, Phoebe. That's why. Oh, God, God, that's why…'

I turn my head away and watch the antelope go back into the forest.

***

I take Amy's Flopsybunny and hide it. I feel bad when she cries for it but then I remember he's her father and I feel glad instead.

***

We've got a new Art teacher. It's better. The old one was always so cross. Ms Peters is different. When I swirl colours together, she tilts her head to one side and says, 'Interesting, Phoebe, very interesting.' Sometimes she takes my picture and pins it to the wall so everyone can see. 'Phoebe likes experimenting with colour,' she says. 'That's important. Until you put them together, you don't know what effect they'll have on one another.'

I duck my head so no one can see my face but I'm pleased all the same.

***

I wake up. It's still so early the corners of my room are thick with shadows. For a moment I think I can see the antelope there, watching me. She's poised for flight, though. I can see it in her eyes, her ears, her delicate,

89

quivering nostrils. 'Don't go,' I say quickly. 'You're safe here,' but she takes no notice and darts away.

In the room across from mine Amy's talking to herself. I get up and go over to my wardrobe where I've got her Flopsybunny hidden. I pull it out and hold it against my cheek for a moment. Then, tightening my mouth, I go in to her room and hold it out to her. 'Look,' I whisper. 'Look what I've found.'

She blinks up at me and then she sits up and laughs. I drop the Flopsybunny in her lap and bend over so I can pick them both up. She's heavier than I thought; it's awkward getting her out of her cot but I manage and we all go back to my room.

'Hey,' I say. 'Hey, Amy, want to see my birds?'

Amy giggles and stretches out her hands. The birds don't mind. They like her. They dip their heads into their seed-cup and watch her with their bright, unwinking eyes.

'Bird,' I say again. 'Bird, Amy.'

Amy purses up her mouth. 'Bir,' she says and then she gets distracted and grabs for my hair.

I lay her down on my bed and tickle her. Mum's wrong. I'm not jealous. I'm not jealous at all. I start to laugh. 'I love you, Amy.' I tell her. 'Look, here's your Flopsybunny. I found him for you, didn't I? I found him for you because I love you.' My voice chokes a bit then and I have to turn my face away. 'I didn't mean to,' I whisper. 'I just…' I can't go on. I'm crying too hard.

Amy's eyes go big and round and she puts her hands up and holds them against my wet cheeks. I snuggle her under my blankets and we lie there a long time until we both fall asleep again.

✳✳✳

Ms Peters reads us a poem for Art.

> 'Tiger, tiger, burning bright
> In the forests of the night,
> What immortal hand or eye
> Could frame thy fearful symmetry?'

I put up my hand. 'Please,' I whisper, 'please read it again.'

'Certainly.'

A thousand images explode behind my eyes. They're not my images, they belong to the poem, mine are quite different. Mine…

Next to me, Gretta Carson asks for a piece of black cartridge paper. 'I want to do it the other way round,' she says. 'White on black.'

Fascinated, I watch her draw white stripes on a black tiger. Her eyes meet mine. 'What's up with you?' She's like her tiger. White face and black eyes and fierce, spiked hair. 'You gunna spend the whole lesson staring at me or what?'

'No. I…' I take a deep breath. 'I like your tiger.'

She shrugs. She doesn't care. She's herself. She doesn't need anyone else.

Sighing, I start to paint the antelope. I have to. She lies in a tangle of slender legs, her head thrown back so you can see her pale, vulnerable throat. Around her I swirl purple and black and silver. I do her eyes last. It's hard to get them right.

'Hey,' says Gretta suddenly. 'Hey, look at you.' Her voice is filled with admiration and I look up at her, surprised.

Jenny and Lucy Barrington come to peer over my shoulder. 'What's that? Hey, everyone, Phoebe Taylor's done an antelope. Of all things. An antelope!'

I spin round. 'Shut up,' I hiss. 'Why don't you just shut up.'

Jenny's laughing. She clutches hold of Lucy and they're both laughing and 'Shut up' I say again and then I slap her.

All of a sudden Ms Peters is there. 'Girls. Girls. Whatever is going on?'

Everyone starts talking at once. Jenny. Lucy. Bethany. Even Gretta. I don't listen. Jenny's got a red mark all down the side of her face. That's enough for me.

I look down at my picture. Very carefully I fold it in half so no one else can see it.

After all my trouble, I did the eyes wrong. The eyes of the antelope aren't sad or bewildered or frightened. Now she's dead, they're just empty.

***

I have to write Jenny a note, apologising. I give it to Ms Peters the next day. 'I don't feel very sorry,' I say. 'But I know I shouldn't have done it.'

Ms Peters nods. She looks sort of sad. I wish she didn't. I'd rather she looked angry.

'She jeered at my painting.'

'I know, but…'

I turn my head away. 'I've never slapped anyone before. I felt bad. As soon as I did it, I felt bad but she shouldn't have…she shouldn't have…' My voice drops to a whisper. 'It felt good too. It felt like I was saving the antelope.'

'Oh, Phoebe, that's not the way. You know that's not the way. 'She puts her hand out and gently turns my face toward her. 'What is it, Phoebe? What's really bothering you? It isn't just the painting. There's something else, isn't there?'

I jerk myself away. 'No. No. Jenny… Jenny laughed at my painting and she…' I stop. I stare at her a moment and then I turn and run out of the room, slamming the door behind me.

***

Gretta comes and sits next to me while I'm eating my lunch. 'Why'd you paint an antelope?' she asks. 'The poem was about a tiger.'

I turn my head away. 'I hate the tiger,' I whisper. 'I couldn't paint him. I had to paint the antelope instead.'

'But…'

'He hunts her,' I say, interrupting. 'Night after night he hunts her. If the poem's about him, it has to be about her too.'

'Tigers have to hunt,' says Gretta, taking a bite out of her sandwich. 'That's not the point, though. The poem's about how fierce and proud the tiger is. Like fire. Like fire in the darkness.'

'I know what the poem's about,' I shout. 'I'm not stupid.'

'Never said you were. I'm interested, that's all.' She puts the rest of her sandwich back in her lunch box and snaps on the lid. 'No one else painted an antelope.'

'That's because…' I stop. It's like with Ms Peters. I don't want to talk about it.

'It was a good painting, though. I wish you had done a tiger, but. I'd have liked to see it.' She's quiet then. Most people look best when they're smiling. Gretta doesn't. Her face is too fierce. She looks best when she frowns.

'You're right,' she says at last. 'Things work in opposites. Black. White. Hunter. Hunted. Good. Bad.'

'The antelope,' I whisper again. 'The antelope.' The word has so much pain in it, I can hardly bear to say it.

Suddenly Gretta laughs. She reaches over and puts her hand on my arm. 'Hey, Phoebe, you've forgotten something, something important. Sometimes the antelope escapes.'

'Escapes…?'

''Course. All the hunted things. Sometimes they escape.' She gets up then and goes back to the classroom.

I don't follow her, though. I stay where I am, scraping patterns in the dirt with the toe of my sneaker

***

The tulips are up in Beatie's garden. I can see the whorls of their leaves through the paling fence. I don't go in to see her though. I want to but she's not on her veranda. She hasn't been all week. It's the cold, I think, and the rain. Or…or perhaps she's gone away. The house looks different…lonely…as if…as if no one cares about it any more…

I hesitate by the gate. I could go up the steps and knock at the door… I can see myself…my hair spilling down the back of my parka…Beatie opening her front door… 'Oh, Lily, how nice to see you. Come in. I've missed you. I've got a fire made up in the lounge and cocoa heating on the stove…'

I bite at my lips. I can't. I can't make myself.

I'm not Lily. The real Lily was a little girl a long time ago. I'm not her. I'm not anyone.

I pick up my back-pack and walk slowly home.

***

93

I don't talk to my birds. He does. Sometimes he comes in when I'm pretending to do my homework and he goes over and whistles to them. I don't care. My birds know about him anyway. They're here at night. Even in the darkness they know what he's doing. He can't fool them.

***

I sit by the window, watching the rain. I used to like doing that. I'd close my eyes and make things into different colours. Bright green rain. Pink grass. A clump of black daffodils. A soft butter-yellow sky. Then I'd turn it into a painting. It was exciting because I never knew quite how it would turn out.

I don't now. It's pointless. I watch my fingers slide down the window-pane. Rain's grey. It's always been grey.

***

He knows. He knows I've changed but he doesn't know why. I don't know why myself.

'You're not thinking of telling, are you, Phoebe? You're not thinking of telling your mother?'

I turn my head away. 'No.'

Suddenly he's angry. 'Look at me,' he hisses. 'Look at me when I'm talking to you.' He grabs my shoulders and forces me to face him. 'She wouldn't believe you anyway.' His mouth twists and he laughs. 'Go on. You'll soon find out. Run and tell her now.'

I wet my lips. 'I wouldn't tell her. She wouldn't care,' I whisper. 'I'd tell...'

His face changes at once. 'You bitch. You little, deceitful bitch.'

I cower away from him but he doesn't notice. He's gone over by the window and he stands there, staring out.

When at last he speaks, he keeps his voice quite steady. 'Tell, Phoebe. Tell and do you know what I'll do? I'll kill your birds. I'll kill your birds and I'll make you watch.'

I catch my breath. He's flexing and unflexing his hands. His hands are so big and my birds, my little, helpless birds...

I stumble to my feet. 'No. No.'

He turns around then. His mouth's smiling but his eyes aren't.

'Please…'

'Oh, Phoebe,' he whispers. 'What's happened to you? You used to be such a sweet little thing. I used to think…' He reaches out his hand as if to touch my cheek but then he draws it back. He straightens up. 'Remember,' he says, 'remember what I've said. I mean it. If you tell, if you tell anyone at all, I'll kill your birds.' He goes then, closing the door behind him.

I sit on my bed staring at the cage on my desk. My birds look like shadows, shadows that hop and flutter from one perch to the next.

***

There's a sign outside Beatie's house. For Sale. Auction on the premises Saturday 15th of October. I read the words over and over again but I can't make them say anything else. I can't make them tell me where Beatie is.

The tulips around the bird bath have stiff red buds. They look just like Beatie said they would.

I walk home very slowly. I don't want to run any more. It was Lily who liked running and Lily has gone. She and Beatie have both gone.

***

I wake up suddenly. Outside, a bird's calling. I lie very still just listening but after a while I get up and go over to the window. The garden's full of shadows but the light's there too, reaching shyly across the lawn, touching for just a moment the red flowers of the tangled grevilleas.

'Yes,' I whisper. 'Yes.'

Panting, I pull aside the fly screen and push the window open. Then, carefully, one by one I catch my birds and let them go. The last one's the worst. Its wings beat so hard against my hands that I almost drop it before I reach the window. Then it's free. It's so small though. Against the immensity of the sky, it's so small, black, a falling black shape cut from paper.

95

***

Sunday afternoon I come back from a walk and when I go into my room, he's sitting there, waiting.

'Where are your birds, Phoebe?' he asks. 'What have you done with them?'

When I don't answer, he grabs hold of me and starts to shout. 'Come on, Phoebe. Tell me.' His breath hisses in his throat. 'You've killed them, haven't you? You've gone and killed them.'

I wrench myself away from him. 'So? You were going to. What difference does it make? You. Me. It doesn't matter. Dead's dead.'

He stares at me, shocked. 'Phoebe…' He sits down on my bed again and puts his hands across his face. 'Oh, Phoebe, what's happened to you? How could you? Those little birds. Those poor little birds.'

I start rearranging the books on my desk. 'Nothing's happened to me,' I say. 'I just didn't want them any more. They were a nuisance.'

I don't turn around but I hear him get to his feet and stumble to the door. I hold myself very still till I'm sure he's gone.

It's almost evening now. In the corner, among the shadows, I see the little antelope lift her head and look at me with wide, compassionate eyes

***

He's avoiding me.

I don't care. I don't care about anything.

Even when he comes at night, he's different. I don't know why. He does the same things, touches me the same way but I know it's different. Perhaps it's better. I can't tell.

***

I wake up and I'm crying. Tiger, tiger, burning bright. Suddenly I want to run to him and tell him the truth about the birds. He said…he said he loved me and sometimes…sometimes…

If he doesn't love me, then…then no one does because my mother… my mother…

96

'I want you to love me,' I whisper. 'Even if…even if…'

The darkness is full of sounds but I can't tell what they are.

'Please. Please. I have to have someone to love me.'

When I fall back to sleep, I dream about the antelope. The tiger's stalking her again. She can't see him because the tasselled grass is stippled through with shadows but she knows he's there. She's not frightened, though. She thinks I can save her. It's in her eyes, her quivering nostrils; she lifts her head and watches me instead of him.

'No,' I tell her. 'You know I can't. He's too powerful and anyway, he's chosen you so you have to…'

Suddenly the tiger springs. Horrified, I watch her sink to her knees and then her eyes glaze over. Everything goes out of them. Hope, recognition, even fear. Herself. Whatever it is that makes her herself, it isn't there any more, it's gone. Roaring, the tiger straddles her body, he lifts his head and his jaws drip with blood.

I take a step or two forward. 'No. No.'

It's too late. A flock of small birds rise screaming from the grass at my feet…

I sit up, confused. Morning. Through the top of my window I can see a glimpse of pale sky. Orange. The sky in my dream was orange and the trees…the antelope stepped out of the dark trees into a little clearing and her eyes…her eyes…

'I could have saved you,' I whisper. 'I could have tried. And if…if both of us…if he'd killed both of us, then at least . .'

I stumble out of bed and reach for my jeans. Inside myself I know what I have to do but it's easier not to think about it.

My mother's in the kitchen, spooning cereal into Amy's mouth. When she sees me, she frowns. 'You all right, Phoebe? You look awfully pale.'

Her concern's so unexpected it almost disarms me. 'I'm fine.' I pour myself a glass of juice but my hands are shaking too much for me to drink it so I set it back down by the sink.

Trust. When she looked at me, the little antelope, her eyes were full of trust.

'Yes,' I whisper. 'Yes.' I turn towards my mother. 'I'm going to school early,' I say aloud. 'I have to. I have to see Ms Peters.'

Mum's still frowning. Her mouth's all pursed up and she looks suddenly uncertain. Amy, her curls sticky with cereal, bangs her spoon against her high chair tray. All at once I can't bear to look at them. Once I've told Ms Peters, then…then…what will happen to us, Mum and Amy and me? Steve? What will happen to Steve…? Oh, tiger, tiger burning bright…

I bite at my lip. I have to. Not for me. For her, for the antelope. I have to give her a chance. My hands are still shaking but I bend down and make them pick up my backpack. 'She's me,' I whisper. 'All this time and it's me, it's really me…' I'm outside now, sunshine, the garden, a bird flying up from the grevilleas and the front door slamming shut behind me.

Burning Bright

I don't like it here.

I didn't like it much at the Sullivans' either but I'd been there a long time so I'd got used to it.

Here it's…I don't know how to put it. I don't mean what it looks like. I could tell you that all right. The family room. The kitchen. The white-tiled bathroom. Even them. Dianne and Mark. The children, Maddie and Liam. It's like one of those magazines. *Better Homes and Gardens. Country Living.* Glossy. That's what they all are. Glossy. None of it's real.

I wish I was back at the Sullivans. They didn't pretend. They didn't particularly like me any more than I liked them but it didn't matter. We understood one another. And Kim. I miss her. Less than a day and already I miss Kim. I take a deep breath and clench my hands because I told Kim I didn't care. 'We aren't really sisters,' I said. 'You were the one that said we were and I told you then it was stupid. We're not even friends.' I felt bad saying that because her face got all pink like she was going to cry but, anyway, she deserved it because the Sullivans are keeping her and not me.

The first thing Dianne says is, 'Philippa? That's right, isn't it?' She makes her eyes crinkle up. 'Hey, I bet all your friends call you Pippa.'

'Pippa's a baby name,' and I watch, smiling, the colour rise in her cheeks.

She shows me my room then. It's right at the back of the house and it's very small but it's got a door that opens up onto the veranda. There's a bed with a yellow doona, an inbuilt wardrobe and a laminated desk with a lamp. The windowsill is as wide as a shelf and it's got things on it, a clock, a little procession of elephants, a pot-plant with striped leaves. I go closer to look at them.

Behind me, Dianne says, 'I put those things there. I hope you don't mind.' She leans forward and picks up one of the elephants. It's got a broken trunk. When she sees me looking at it, she flushes again and puts it down. 'They're only old things. You can put some of your own things there instead if you like…'

I don't answer so she goes over to the desk and straightens the lamp a bit. She's got her head bent so I can't see her face but her hands give her away, they're all jumpy like a little kid's and at last she says, 'Well, I'll leave you to unpack and settle in. Call me if you need anything.'

I sit on the bed and stare down at my own hands. They look wrong. They're too big and the skin around my nails is rough and broken.

Suddenly I jump up and tip everything out of my back-pack. Underclothes. T-shirts. Jeans. The denim jacket Mrs Sullivan got me from the op shop. Right at the bottom there's the shoebox with my special things. Nothing much. The metal horse I stole from a monopoly set. A bottle of coloured sand. A blue enamelled butterfly on a leather thong. Some origami cranes. A new colouring-in book and a packet of textas. Kim bought me those. I open the plastic envelope that holds the textas and let them spill out onto the bed. Then I flick through the pages of the book until I find the right picture. A bunch of poppies. 'Grey,' I say. 'Grey and black.' I hear Kim's voice protesting in my mind. It's like she's here in the room with me. I frown at her to make her go away but then I remember that she used up all her pocket money on me. 'All right,' I say. 'All right, Kim, I'll do one pink. One whole pink flower just for you.'

It's too much. Remembering Kim is too much. I fling myself forward on the bed and bite at my knuckles to stop myself from crying.

✳✳✳

Maddie stands at my door. 'Mum says tea's ready.'

'I don't want any.'

She's got eyes like Kim. They show everything she feels.

'You deaf or something? Go away.'

'Mum says…' Her lips quiver but she's resolute. 'Come on. It's barbecue. We're having it in the garden and Mum's made a cake for you. A chocolate cake.'

'I said…'

Suddenly she notices my colouring-in book on the floor. 'Oh, look.'

She's got hold of it now and she's all excited, jigging from one leg to the other. 'Can I do some? After, can I do some with you? It's my best thing, colouring in, and Ms Roberts said...'

I wrench the book from her. 'Give that here. It's mine.'

'I was just looking.'

'Well, don't.' I stand up and comb my fingers through my hair. I'll have to go with her. If I don't, Dianne will come and Mark... 'What are you standing there staring for? I thought you said tea was ready,' and I march off down the passage and into the kitchen.

Through the open sliding doors I can see them in the garden, Mark and Dianne at the bricked-in barbecue, Liam staggering across the patio cradling a red balloon.

Maddie pushes past me and runs to join them. It's like she knows she belongs there. A photograph. The perfect family. All smiling at one another.

I turn suddenly and run back to my room and slam the door.

I knew it would be bad. I just didn't know it would be as bad as this.

***

I work out what to do about school. When Rosemary comes on Monday, I show her the bus timetable. 'Look,' I say. 'All I have to do is catch the bus to the Interchange, then the O-bahn to the city and then...'

Rosemary bites at her lip. 'Oh, Philippa, I don't think so. I...'

'Please,' I whisper. 'Just till the end of the year. I'd have to leave then anyway because of high school.'

She's stopped listening, though. I can tell by her face. She's the other Rosemary now, the Department one, Rosemary Cookson, social worker. 'I've just been to Beechwood Primary,' she says. 'It's a good school. You'll like it there.'

'I won't. I told you. I have to go back to Acacia Park.'

'Philippa...'

'They know me there. They leave me alone.' My hands twist themselves together in my lap. 'I'm too old to be in grade seven. You know I am. The other kids my age are already at high school.'

'Is that what this is all about?' She laughs a bit. 'You don't need to worry. I explained everything to the principal, Ms Weston. She's going to talk to your class. She's very understanding…'

I don't want to hear any more. I turn my head away and stare out of the window. Along the fence, Dianne's got some sort of bush growing. It's got weird, red flowers that look like they belong in the sea. 'Tentacles,' I whisper to myself. 'Flowers with tentacles.' I duck my head so Rosemary can't see my face and make pictures in my mind. They flaunt themselves, those flowers. They don't care what anyone else thinks. And red's a good colour. A good fierce colour. A warning colour.

***

I wake up and I don't feel too bad. Another foster home. Another school. I've done it all before. I reach for my jeans and denim jacket. The jacket's too big. It always has been but that's why I like it. It hides my body. If it wasn't for my hair, I'd look like a boy. I pull it back and study my face in the wardrobe mirror. I'm not sure if I've got a boy's face or not. I think my mouth's wrong. When I'm not frowning, my lips look too full. I shake my head and let my hair fall back round my shoulders. I'd get it cut but it's a bit curly. Short it would be worse. I remember from when I was little. 'Such pretty hair,' Mr Moffat would say and then his eyes would go sly and he'd reach out to touch my cheek. I zip up my jacket and pick up my backpack.

'I'm not going to school with you and Maddie,' I tell Dianne when I've finished my toast and orange juice. 'I'm going by myself.'

'Oh, but Philippa…'

'I know the way. Mark showed me last night.'

'But I thought…' She's got sandwich stuff all over the bench, sliced beef and tomatoes and an opened jar of pickles. 'Well, if you're sure…'

'I'm not a little kid. I don't need you to hold my hand.'

She presses her lips together but she doesn't say anything.

I push back my chair.

Her hands are jumpy again. 'Your lunch-box. Here's your lunch-box. There's a bottle of juice too in case you get thirsty.'

'Orange and mango,' interrupts Maddie. 'I put them in the fridge last night to get cold.' Her voice gets louder and she juts out her bottom lip. 'I want you to come with us,' she says. 'You're my sister now and sisters…'

I whirl around. 'Shut up,' I shout. 'Who told you that?' I grab the lunch-box from Dianne and make for the door.

I feel better once I reach the school gates. Calm. A couple of kids stare at me but I make myself stare back till they get embarrassed and look away.

I find the front office and go up the steps. 'I'm Philippa Matthews.' It sounds right. Belligerent. I nod to myself and wait for Ms Weston to take me to my classroom.

'Philippa's joining us from Acacia Park Primary School,' she says when we get there. 'I hope you will all make her feel welcome.'

So that's over. I slide thankfully into a seat at the back and busy myself with my books. A girl turns round to whisper to me but I look away and don't answer. Girls. I know all about them. Friendly smiles and mean eyes. They're worse than boys. Cleverer.

My hands start to clench themselves under the desk. It's like I'm little again. For just a moment I think I can hear them laughing at me. Circle of faces and me in the middle. Sticks and stones may break your bones but names will never hurt you. Mrs Sullivan told me that when I first went to live with them. She said it with her mouth all pursed up so I knew she thought it was my fault. Everything. The names. The fights. The bruises on my arms and legs. Jason Dickson's black eye. The broken window at the supermarket. I lift my head and stare hard at the blackboard. It doesn't matter now. I'm bigger. They'll leave me alone. Or if they don't, they soon will. I know how to take care of myself. I haven't forgotten. I haven't forgotten anything.

After recess, it's German. I'm surprised. I thought they left things like that till high school. She's all soft and pretty, the German teacher, and we have to call her Fraulein. She goes from desk to desk giving out a vocab sheet. I don't even bother looking at mine. I turn it over and start drawing horses instead. Horses make a landscape more beautiful. I heard someone say that once. I don't know why. I think it was part of a poem. It doesn't matter. I like it. I like saying it to myself. It makes my horses come alive. I do them very simple like a cave painting. It's amazing how it works, a swirl, a half-line, mane and tail…they're running free, mare and stallion, arched necks and pounding hooves and behind them a little faltering foal…

Even when the teacher raps on her table and calls the class to attention, I take no notice. I'm not there.

'My true self,' I whisper. 'My true self is running with the horses.'

Mrs Sullivan was wrong. Words have a power all of their own.

***

I sit cross-legged on my bed with the box of matches I stole from the supermarket. I like matches. I like the way they flare up when you strike them. The flame's alive. It runs along the wood, so eager, but before it reaches my fingers it flickers out and dies so I have to quickly strike another one. All the flames are different. Some of them are like soldiers; they stand up and you can see inside them to their blue translucent hearts but others quiver sideways, they curl like the tentacles of Dianne's flowers. It's sad when they go out though. It doesn't matter how fiercely they burn, when they go out, it's sad.

If…if…I feel my eyes go wide and imagine the night sky full of leaping, dancing flames, orange and crimson and gold, oh! gold, gold and the darkness, the darkness'd be lit up so everyone could see. They'd be free, we'd all be free and I, I…

Very carefully I put all the burnt matchsticks back in their box and hide it under the textas in my shoebox.

***

I take Liam for a walk in his stroller. He's been crying. He doesn't like childcare. I try to tell Dianne but she won't listen. She doesn't care. You have to fit. If you're not the right shape to fit in the pattern they've made for you, they cut and hammer and bend you till you do. When I think that, I start to shudder. It's like at night when I wake up from a dream I can't quite remember. It's like I know in the end they'll make me into something I'm not.

I open the gate and carefully negotiate the stroller down the slope of the driveway. Liam's heavier than he looks. He's got his silky and he's rubbing it against his cheek and talking to it. Not proper talking of course, he's too young for that. It's like birdsong, I think, no, no, water in

104

a creek, water over stones, smooth, brown stones and the water very clear except where it's laced with foam. The picture gets inside my mind and makes me calm again.

I look up. It's proper spring now. The street trees have begun to uncurl their leaves. They look like alien hands, the leaves, all pale with little fluttery fingers. I slow down so Liam can look at everything.

'Sparrows,' I say, pointing. 'Sparrows on the lawn.' The garden trees aren't like the street trees. They're smaller and some of them droop with flowers. 'Oh, Liam, look, a pretty-pretty tree.'

A few houses up we can hear a dog barking.

'Gog,' says Liam suddenly. 'Goggie.'

For some reason, I feel a sudden rush of joy. 'Yes,' I say. 'Dog. Let's go and find him.' My voice isn't like mine at all. It's like the spring's got inside of me too. 'Leaves,' I think. 'It's like something inside of me is putting out leaves.'

I start to run. I hold on tight to the stroller and start to run in the direction of the barking dog.

***

I sit on my bed and turn the pages of my colouring-in book till I find the right picture. Giraffes. An elongated palm tree. I close my eyes so I can concentrate. It's always hard finding the right colours. Until you see them together, you don't know if they'll work or not. Blue, I decide, sky-blue and, excited, I start to fill in the giraffe's neck. I nod to myself and very carefully do the spots magenta.

It takes me a long time to finish but when I do I feel satisfied. I get ready for bed and all the time the colours are there dancing together in my mind. They stay with me till at last I fall asleep.

***

The dreams come back. I don't know why. I haven't had them for years. Not since I stopped being a little kid.

The dreams aren't about anything real. Darkness. Closed in darkness .Mummy. I can't breathe. Please. Please, Mummy. She doesn't come. I can't remember her, my mother, but she was in the dream and if she'd come, if only she'd come I'd be safe, I know I'd be safe… Except…except…it isn't true. I know it isn't. The dream and my mother and being frightened are all mixed up together and I know it's better if I don't remember.

After a while I get up. I stumble across to my desk and the hidden box of matches. They're hard to open, the box seems to jerk in my hands but I've got one, I've got a match and in a moment it's alight, the flame leaps up, quivering, red and gold and yellow. It's alive and the darkness, the darkness…

'Burning bright,' I whisper. 'Oh, burning bright.' It's another poem, I think confused, we did it at school at the beginning of the year. Tiger, tiger! burning bright / In the forests of the night… It doesn't matter about the rest of it. Not for us. The tiger and me and the dancing, dancing flame, we're burning bright together and that way we're safe, all of us safe and the darkness around us can't hurt us.

****

It's my birthday. October the sixth. I'm fourteen. I straighten my shoulders and stare at my face in the mirror. Fourteen's a good number. Eleven. Twelve. Thirteen. They're little kid numbers. Fourteen. Fifteen. Sixteen. They're different. They've got power.

I go into the kitchen for breakfast. Mark has already gone to work and Dianne doesn't say anything but Maddie's all sparkly like she's got a secret. I stare at her until her cheeks go pink and she drops her head, embarrassed. They've got something planned and she's been told not to tell. I don't care. It's enough for me that I'm getting older. Being grown-up can't be worse than being a kid.

I get home late. I do that now summer's coming. Wander round the streets a bit after school. I like looking at things. Gardens. Birds. A park with a stone fountain. The mutilated street trees. They make me shudder, though, so I concentrate instead on the patterns their leaves make on the ground. I stop and watch them and it's like I'm remembering something. Damp earth and the smell of something sweet and…and…someone singing…my mother…my mother singing… I shake my head impatiently. The other things. I can remember them all right. My grandmother. Mr Moffat coming into my room at night and his hands, his hands… I bite down hard on my lip. I don't want to remember that. My mother. I want to remember my mother. I clench my hands. I'm fourteen now. I don't need her. I don't need anyone.

When I get home, Dianne's made a bit of a party for me. She's even got Rosemary to come. I feel stupid. Everyone looking at me. They've got the table all fancy with bought flowers and dishes of party food, corn chips and peanuts and little pizzas made like pinwheels. Right in the middle they've got a chocolate cake with strawberries and striped candles.

'Light the candles! Light the candles!' shrieks Maddie, jumping up and down. 'Then you can make a wish. Oh, Philippa, what'll you wish for? I know what Daddy's bringing home for you so I hope it's that, I hope it's…' She stops suddenly and puts her hand over her mouth. 'Oh, Mummy, I almost told and I promised I wouldn't.'

I don't say anything. I take the box of matches from Rosemary and start to light the candles. It changes us immediately, the candles. Dianne pulls the curtains across the sliding doors and our faces go solemn with wonder.

I lift Liam out of his high chair. 'Want to help blow them out?' I whisper so only he can hear. 'Want to help make the magic happen?'

Mark rushes in then. He nods to Rosemary. 'Sorry I'm late. I told Dianne not to make you all wait.' He's got a flat package in his hand, all wrapped up in coloured paper. 'For you, Philippa. For the birthday girl. For our birthday girl.' He laughs a bit then and Dianne comes over to put her arm around me.

I pull myself away and they're all looking at me and Maddie's shouting, 'Hurry. Oh, Philippa, you're so slow.'

I duck my head and fumble with the ribbon bows but I can't undo them so in the end I just tear them off.

It's a silver bracelet, all cut out in shapes like lace. I don't know what to say. My throat starts to get tight so I take it out of its box and hold it up for everyone to see.

Afterwards, when I'm alone in my room, I put it in my box with my other things. I sit on my bed for a long time with my hands in my lap. There's too many feelings inside me and I don't know what to do with them. I bite at my lip. I want them to go away. Some of them are good feelings but I still want them to go away.

***

I tip the bracelet out on my desk and stir it round with one finger. I can't keep it. I know I can't.

Mr Moffat used to give me things. A doll that fitted into a match-box. A hairclip shaped like a butterfly. A green glass frog.

I don't trust presents. Not ones that are meant to make me feel special. Mark isn't like Mr Moffat, I know that. But he and Dianne still want something from me.

I take the bracelet out into the garden and bury it near the bush with the red flowers.

***

The afternoon's gone on too long. I glance around me. All the other kids are busy with their projects. Ancient Egypt. I don't like the ancient Egyptians. The things they draw are ugly especially when it's their gods

I push back my chair and stand up. When the teacher frowns at me, I mutter, 'I have to go to the toilet,' and, before she can answer, I'm out the door, grabbing up my back-pack as I go. I'm free. The words go round and round inside me and I have to whirl with them until I'm dizzy and breathless.

Panting, I lean against a street tree and watch, behind its leaves, the wild spinning of the sky.

At last I push back my hair and make for the bus stop. I'm going to see Kim. I'm surprised. It's there in my mind, the idea of seeing Kim, as if I've been thinking about it for a long time. Perhaps I have. Perhaps you can think things without knowing it.

It's a long way. Somehow that makes it more exciting. The bus. The O-bahn. Another bus. I squeeze my eyes shut for a moment. I feel like I'm a little kid out for a treat.

My mood changes a bit, though, when I reach the street where the Sullivans live. I'm not sure about seeing them again. But Kim. She's like Maddie. She's…'all lit up inside, sky-bright', I whisper and I start to run.

She's not there. I'm too early. I drop my backpack and stare at Mrs Sullivan. 'But…'

'School's only just out. What did you expect?' Suddenly her eyes

108

narrow. 'What are you doing here anyway? You haven't started running away again, have you? Those new people, they know you're here?'

I turn my head away. The door frame needs painting. You can see the old colour where the paint's flaked off. Grey, it used to be grey but they've painted it over dark green.

'Can I come in and wait?' I ask. 'She shouldn't be much longer, should she?' I don't sound like myself. Subdued, I sound subdued. I take a deep breath and lift my head. 'Kim's my sister,' I shout. 'None of you can change that. Not you or Rosemary or…' I stop.

Her expression hasn't changed.

'I'll wait round the front,' I say. 'You don't have to worry. I'm not expecting to stay.'

'Philippa…'

I toss my head. 'I prefer to wait round the front.'

Her face goes a bit pink then and she bites at her lip but her eyes don't change and I know she's relieved she won't have to have me inside where she'd have to talk to me and pretend to be friendly.

I pick up my bag and go back to the gate. They've got a stone wall there and I hoist myself up onto it.

Kim comes a bit later. She's got Jenny and Esmay with her and another girl I don't know and they keep stopping and clutching hold of one another and giggling. When she sees me, she hesitates. I wait for her to shout 'Philippa' and come running but she doesn't. Instead she turns and says something to the other girls and then comes on by herself. She's changed. Even before she gets up to me, I know. She looks the same but inside herself she's grown up.

I feel suddenly very cold and I pull up the collar of my jacket and hunch down inside it.

'I didn't know you were coming,' she says. 'Mum didn't say.'

'Mum? What do you mean Mum?'

'Oh,' she says and then she laughs. Even her laughter's changed. It's lost something, something real. It's brittle, I think confused, brittle like glass and if it shatters, then…then…

I lift my head and I think there is something in my face because she says in a thin, little-girl voice. 'Didn't Mum tell you? They're going to adopt me. They're just waiting for the final papers from the court.'

'You can't let them do that. You know about your parents. You can remember them. You told me.'

'My parents are dead. They aren't here now and George and Mavis love me. They told me.'

'That doesn't make any difference. How can it? You'd be pretending… that's what you'd be doing pretending and…'

She gets angry then. Her cheeks go pink and she stamps her foot. 'I wouldn't be. You don't know. You don't know anything about it.'

'I do. Of course I do.' I jump down from the wall and grab hold of her arm. 'Don't you see? What's happened in the past's important. You can't just change it and make George and Mavis your parents. Everything that's happened, your mother and father getting killed in the accident, it's there inside you. It makes you who you are…'

She laughs and her eyes go mean. It shocks me, Kim's eyes going small and mean…

'You're jealous,' she says. 'You're jealous because they're adopting me and not you.'

I slap her. I can't help it. My hand goes out and does it and I'm glad. I slap her again and again and the whole side of her face goes red and I'm glad, I'm glad because it spoils her, it makes her look blotched and ugly. It makes her look like me.

'Baby,' I say. 'Look at the baby. You're crying, Kim. You're crying like a baby. Aren't you going to run in and tell Mummy? You've got a mummy now, haven't you? You've got a mummy to tell.'

'Philippa,' she whimpers. 'Philippa.'

Her eyes, wet-lashed, are Bambi eyes and I think, for one heart-stopping moment I think she might be the old Kim, the one who wanted me to be her sister, but I'm crying too so I can't wait to find out and I run past her and down the street though she keeps on calling my name over and over again.

***

I know what I'm going to do. I don't even have to think about it. Kerosene. Newspaper. Another box of matches. I arrange and rearrange the words in my mind. They're not as beautiful as the words from the tiger poem but they mean the same thing.

110

Saturday evening I pack everything into the back of Liam's stroller. 'I'm just taking Liam for his walk,' I call out to Dianne in the kitchen. 'It's been so hot today he'll like a walk before he goes to sleep.'

Maddie looks up from her book. 'Can I come too?'

'No.'

'You don't like me, do you? You only like Liam.'

'So? That's your bad luck, isn't it?'

Her mouth quivers but I don't care. She's nothing to me.

Outside, the colour's draining out of the sky except for behind the hills where it's all bruised by the setting sun.

'Come on, Liam.' I say. 'We've got a lot to do before dark.'

'Gog?' he says. 'Goggie?'

'Not tonight. Tonight we're going somewhere else. We're going to school.'

The school feels different with no one there. Not empty. Abandoned. I shake back my hair and push Liam through the side gate. In front of us there's the oval, a scrubby garden of wattles and drooping bottlebrush and right at the end, a line of temporary, wooden classrooms. I park Liam under a tree.

'Here,' I say, giving him his silky. 'You hold that and wait for me. I won't be long.'

He rubs his silky against his cheek. Above it his eyes are big and solemn and…trusting, I think, and something starts to ache inside me. I bite at my lip and jerk my head away but only for a moment. I grab up my bag and run over to the classrooms. It's very quiet. Just my footsteps on the gravel, a whisper of wind, a bird, and over everything, the wide darkening sky.

With a little cry, I pick up a rock and hurl it through the nearest window. I stand back and watch it explode into fragments that twist and spin as they catch the light. Stars. My throat goes tight. They look like stars. When the stars threw down their spears / And watered heaven with their tears. That's in the poem too, the tiger poem, and my heart beats inside me, steady and relentless, the tiger in the forests of the night…

When I've finished, I don't look back. I don't have to. I run to Liam. 'Come on, 'I say. 'We have to hurry now.' I grab the handle of the stroller and run with it to the gate.

Behind me. Behind me I know the little dancing flames are reaching, reaching out to the sky, gold, gold a sunburst of gold. I stop for a moment to catch my breath. It doesn't matter. My mother. Mr Moffat. Kim. Maddie. None of them matter. 'Burning bright,' I whisper, shuddering. 'Oh, Liam, burning bright.'

I cross the road into Whitmore Avenue and, still without looking back, take him home.

In the Forests of the Night

It's morning. I don't want it to be. Not yet. I keep my eyes closed but the light prickles against my eyelids and I have to put my hands across my face to block it out. Jack's talking on the telephone. I can tell by the rise and fall of his voice. I can't hear the words, though. I feel my heart slow down. It's all right. I can't hear the words. I reach back to the darkness inside me and watch it swirl around me. I start to lose myself in it but it's too late.

Jack's there. He's got hold of my shoulder and he's shaking me. 'Lena. Wake up.'

Owl, I think, confused; the owl who hunts by night and all the little, big-eyed creatures with me shudder and clutch at one another.

'Come on, Lena. Wake up.'

'No, I…' It isn't any use, though. In the end I have to open my eyes.

'Maeve's coming,' Jack says, going over to the mirror and straightening his tie. 'I rang her. She's coming at ten with Cynthia. You'll have to get up.'

I hold my hands out in front of my face. They dart and swoop together like birds in flight. I concentrate on the patterns they make and feel myself begin to smile.

But Jack won't leave us alone. 'Maeve and Cynthia are going to take you out,' he says. 'The zoo, I think. They've promised Cynthia's little girl. You'll like that, won't you, Lena, something different.'

'I don't want…'

'Oh, Lena, stop it. It'll be fun. You always liked Cynthia. You said, when you were growing up, your cousin Cynthia was just like your sister.'

His voice makes me frown. It's got too many feelings in it.

He comes over and sits down on the bed next to me. 'Lena, you don't want to go back to the hospital, do you? You promised, you promised if I brought you home last time, you promised you'd try.' He's got one of my hands now and he's chafing it gently between his own. 'Please, Lena. Please try.'

I turn my face away. 'All right, Jack.' I whisper. 'All right. I'll go with Auntie Maeve when she comes.' It isn't my voice. It can't be. It's a child's, the little girl Lena who always did what other people wanted.

I wait until Jack goes to work before I get up. It's very quiet. The clock ticking. A bird in the garden. The sudden rush of water when I turn on the shower. I wrap myself in a towel and go slowly back to the bedroom. The light comes in through the venetian blinds and falls in stripes across the bed. I hesitate, fascinated, but then I remember and turn wearily to my dressing table. A pair of lacy briefs. A bra. I open my wardrobe. None of my clothes look familiar. Beige skirts, a silk blouse, an impossibly tailored suit with wide shoulders, a cashmere sweater. I shake my head. At the back I find a blue dress with pearl buttons and a little crocheted collar. It looks like something my mother would have worn but I pull it out and slip it over my head. It feels safe.

I fluff my hair out around my face and stare at my reflection in the mirror. 'Crowd,' I say. 'You're just Crowd.' I feel like a little girl in a school play. 'You're not the star. It doesn't matter what you do. No one's going to notice.'

My eyes don't quite believe me but I tighten my mouth and glare back at them till, abashed, they veil themselves behind my lashes. Stockings. Black strap sandals. I straighten my collar one last time and go into the lounge to wait for Cynthia and Auntie Maeve.

They're late. I don't mind. I sit very still and stare at my hands in my lap. The silence around me is as still as glass. It locks me in. Safe. A tower of glass and I'm safe inside it. Then, before I can catch my breath, they're there. I stare at them, confused. Cynthia's mouth is too red. She's laughing but her eyes, sly, watch me and they don't laugh. I have to hide myself in Maeve's embrace. They've left the little girl in the car. Alice. Abbey. Amelia. I can never remember her name. It doesn't matter. Ruth. The suddenness of it pierces me. If I'd had a little girl, I'd have called her Ruth. Jack didn't want children though. He said… I shake my head and try to smile.

They bustle me out to the car. 'You sit in the back with Abbey, lovie. There's more room there.'

I nod and get in. I fumble with the seat-belt buckle. I can't get the catch to work but they don't notice so I hold it together with my hand. The little girl's in the corner opposite. She's thin, ungainly, all jutting elbows and staring eyes. I don't care. I don't like little girls. I turn my head away and look out of the window.

A drooping street tree. A boy on a bicycle. A mongrel dog. We slow down. We're in the city proper now. Traffic lights. A confusion of cars. We jolt forward, turn, the bridge, below us a glimpse of the river, a tangle of willows and a pair of black swans with a family of bedraggled cygnets. I let my breath out with a little gasp. Ahead though's the zoo. The walls are too high. I'd forgotten that. The walls tipped with vicious little spikes and behind it, behind it… My hands, frightened, clench themselves in my lap.

But Cynthia's parked the car. She gets out and slams the door. 'Come on, Lena, Abbey. Oh, Mum, what are you fussing with now?'

Maeve's gone round to the boot. She's unloading an esky, a couple of fold-up chairs, a blanket. 'I just thought, while we're so close to the park here, a bit of a picnic, then we'll have all afternoon for the zoo, eh, Abbey?'

The child doesn't answer but her mouth tightens imperceptibly. She's disappointed, I think; she's tired of waiting but she's careful not to show it. Nine, ten years old and already she's learned… Something shudders inside me. Oh, Ruth, Ruth…

It doesn't take long. Paper plates of chicken and salad. Home-made lemonade. The little girl's flung herself down on the grass under a tree, arms outstretched, hunched knees, a fan of dark hair; the tree makes leaf-shadows across her face.

'Abbey, sit up and eat your lunch.'

I turn my face away. Cynthia's voice is just like my mother's.

As soon as we've repacked the car, we cross the road to the zoo.

I concentrate on putting one foot in front of the other. If I don't look up, if I…I clutch at Maeve's arm. 'Maeve, I don't think…'

'What is it, lovie? Come on, Cynthia's getting the tickets for all of us. Look, they've still got this old turnstile. Do you remember when you were little? You and Cynthia always loved the zoo. Every holidays you'd both beg me to take you and in the end I'd have to give in…'

I look around me, dazed. It's a different world. The bars around the enclosures, cruel as spears, but the light is so gentle, it seems hazed with gold…

'Flamingoes,' I say slowly. 'I remember the flamingoes…'

'And the peacocks,' says Cynthia, turning. 'A keeper gave us some feathers once. You wouldn't let anyone touch yours, Lena. You thought the colours would come off like they do on butterfly wings.' Suddenly she jerks around. 'Abbey. Where's Abbey?'

My mouth's dry. The little girl. Oh, the little girl. It's like at night when the owl comes, when…

But Maeve's there, her arm is still around me, steadying me. 'She's over there, Cynthia. By the antelopes.'

Cynthia's mouth twists. 'Should have expected it. Always off mooning over something.' She turns to me. 'Reminds me of you, Lena. Bit of a worry, eh?'

I try to make myself smile at her, friends, Cynthia and I, little girls together with our peacock feathers, but my lips are too stiff so I turn my head away and follow Maeve across to the antelopes. There are eight or nine of them all bunched together, pale brown with slender black-marked legs and wide dark eyes. At our approach, the child turns. She's tucked her hair behind her ears and her face is thin and plain enough to be my own.

She runs to her mother and drags at her arm. 'Come and see,' she says. 'Oh, I do like them. I like them best.'

'You haven't seen anything else yet. What about the elephant? Or the zebra? Or the monkeys? Everyone likes the monkeys.'

She lifts her chin. 'They're ordinary,' she says. 'Everyone knows about them. Not like blackbuck. That's what they're called –blackbuck. Oh, I do think…'

But Cynthia's lost patience. 'Come on. We've got a lot to see. Your gran will make us stop soon for a cup of tea. What'll it be first, Abbey? Hurry and make up your mind. Bears? Giraffe? The big cats? Your Auntie Lena will want to see them. Remember Mum? Remember how Lena was so frightened of the lions and tigers but she couldn't keep away. Don't look, you'd say, if it upsets you don't look. But she wouldn't listen, though afterwards…'

'It was the poem,' I say before I can stop myself. 'The poem we did at school. "Tiger, tiger, burning bright." I thought, I thought if I watched the tiger long enough, I'd understand it, I'd understand the poem…'

Cynthia laughs. 'And did you, Lena? Did you understand it?'

'No because… Did He who made the lamb make thee? I could never understand why. Why He made the tiger when…'

Cynthia doesn't answer. Perhaps she didn't hear me. Or…or perhaps I didn't actually say it. Sometimes I think I say things when I don't.

They've gone on ahead of me. My mind whirls with images. What the hammer? What the chain? No, not that. The gentle bit. When the stars threw down their spears. I always liked that. The newborn stars weeping over the creation of the doomed world. Oh, God, God, not beauty and terror but pity. Christ weeping over Jerusalem. Oh, love is too hard, it wants you to care too much but pity…pity might be easier…

The little girl comes back and catches hold of my hand. 'We won't look at the tiger if you don't want to.'

'I don't mind. Cynthia got it wrong. She always…' I stop.

Her eyes are wide and dark. Antelope eyes, I think, and my heart shudders again in recognition. Sighing, I follow her to where Maeve and Cynthia are waiting.

My head aches. There's too much to see. A red and blue macaw. A lemur with black-rimmed eyes. A gnu calf staggering after its mother. The gilded dome of the elephant house. The little girl darts forward. The elephant stands in the bare yard moving delicately from one foot to another, its head swinging, its eyes infinitely tired. 'Oh,' I whisper, 'oh,' and Maeve says, 'Look. Abbey, look at the elephant dancing.'

She's not fooled. 'That's not dancing, Gran. It's too sad for dancing.' Her breath catches in her throat. 'Oh, why doesn't it stop? Why doesn't it stop?'

My lips quiver. I know why it doesn't stop but Cynthia's watching me so I fumble with my handbag and don't say anything.

The Nocturnal House. Bettongs. A spotted quoll. A pixie-faced bat. A white owl. My hands clutch at one another and I turn quickly away.

The little girl's at my elbow. 'Don't you like owls either, Auntie Lena?'

'They're predators.' My voice is so loud she flinches in surprise but now I've started I can't stop. 'They don't look like it. Not like hawks and eagles. They look cruel, with their beaks and talons but the owl's just the

same. It's worse because it hunts at night when all the little creatures…
They think they're safe, safe in the darkness but they're not, they're not.'

'But that's what owls do. They hunt. Otherwise they'd starve.' She
leans forward and puts her hand against the glass. 'They don't like it in
here. The animals. They should set them free. All of them.'

I laugh harshly. 'All of them?' I grab her shoulder and shake her.
'What would happen then? They'd let the tiger loose and your antelope.
What then? Your antelope with her heart torn out and the tiger all striped
with blood.'

'Lena…' Maeve's stepped forward, she's putting out a restraining
hand, but the little girl's lifted her head; in the flickering, bluish light her
face is vague and indistinct but I can still see the shining of her eyes.

'They can't help it,' she insists. 'They are what they are. They have
to…' Her voice quivers to a stop. 'I like the antelope best. I told you. But
the tiger's beautiful too. He can't help what he is.' She breaks away from
me. She's crying, I think, and I feel my throat go tight with pity.

'Ruth,' I whisper. 'Oh, Ruth.'

Then we're outside again. The sky's changed, though. All the gold's
gone from the afternoon. The paths are striped with lengthening shadows.

I hear my voice rise. 'Take me home. Maeve, Maeve, I've had enough.
I want to go home.'

'A cup of tea,' says Maeve quickly. 'That's what you need, lovie, a nice
cup of tea. We'll go over to the tea rooms, Cynthia, and wait for you and
Abbey there.'

I don't say anything. I want to. I want to tell her about the tiger in
the forests of the night but I'm too tired. Oh, hunter and hunted and
both are stained with blood. I don't understand it. Because if the hunter
can't help it, maybe…maybe…all the little creatures of the night huddling
together, waiting, and the antelope, the antelope lift their delicate heads
and watch the tiger stalk them through the long grass. Innocent. All
innocent. Hunter and hunted together. Maybe that's what it means. Did
He who made the Lamb make Thee?

I let Maeve lead me to a table by the window and sit down in the chair
she indicates. 'Ruth,' I whisper, 'Ruth,' and I hear her say again, 'We are
what we are,' and I take a deep breath and wait for Maeve to return with
our tea.

The Lamb

In the evening when the colour of the sky has deepened, Jamie and his mother go down to shut up the chooks. The grass under the fruit trees is furtive with shadows and Jamie hesitates. He doesn't like shadows. They remind him of night and the all-enveloping darkness.

Mum's told him. Over and over, she's told him. 'It's all right. He's not coming back. I promise, Jamie. This time your father's not coming back.'

Except…except…in the darkness it's real again. Shouting. Slammed doors. His mother's bruised face. It's happened before, his father leaving. And he's come back. In the end he's always come back and, however good it is to begin with, sooner or later he changes into the other father, the one who's angry, the one who…

Mum pushes open the gate. 'Come on, Jamie. They're not all in yet. We'll have to wait.'

Jamie sits next to his mother on an upturned trough and looks around him. He likes watching things. Wind in the leaves. The grazing sheep. The sunset sky. A pair of crested pigeons by the feed-shed. The hens, in stops and starts, come up from the edge of the scrub, the rooster strutting importantly behind them. They cluster in front of the open door until one, bolder than the rest, darts inside and the rest follow.

Mum gets up to shut them in. 'Good. That's done. We'd better check on the sheep.' She climbs over the fence and holds the top wire down so Jamie can scramble after her. The light that is almost defeated in the sky and the surrounding scrub lies across the paddock in a thick golden haze.

Jamie stops suddenly. 'Mum, Mum. Look. Nadia isn't there.'

Mum glances over at the little huddle of sheep. 'You're right. She must have gone off to have her lamb.'

'Why? Why doesn't she stay with the others? They wouldn't mind.'

'She wants to be alone.'

They find Nadia under the trees at the beginning of the scrub. When they approach her, she turns her head to stare at them but she doesn't move away. Jamie can see on the ground the places where she's lain down and got up again. She looks suddenly so small. He feels his breath tighten in his chest and he has to put his arms around himself to hold himself still.

'She'll be a while yet.' Mum frowns up at the sky. 'Once it's dark, foxes will come. They did last year.' She reaches out to put an arm around Jamie. 'Not this year, though. I'll not let them get any lambs this year.'

'But how…how can you…'

Mum's mouth goes tight. 'We'll put her in the shed. As soon as the lamb's born, we'll put them both in the shed.' She stops and bites at her lip. 'I'll have to go back to the house to get a torch.'

'I could get it.'

'I'm not sure where it is. I'll have to look and… Oh, Jamie do you think you could stay here instead and…and watch.' Her words, too eager, start to fall over one another. 'She'd be all right if you were here even if it took me a while and they won't come, I'm sure they won't come if you're with her.' She touches his cheek and smiles, her face for one moment enticingly like his grown-up sister Lauren's and then she's gone, swallowed up by the shadows around the sheds, the wooden gate, the line of fruit trees leading up to the house.

He hears the dog bark, a car door slam, Lauren's voice, high and excited, and then there's nothing but the silence and Nadia and the tremulous beating of his own heart.

He turns his head. Against the red-stained sky the trees are very black as if they have been cut from paper. Beneath them, in the pooled darkness, he can just make out Nadia, the outline of her drooping head, her ears, the glint of her narrow eyes. A shudder goes through her. Jamie sees it and shudders with her. He knows about birth. Wonder. Delight. Magic of chicken from egg, once, breathless, a butterfly, wet-winged, from its chrysalis, poppies, even the cream and gold poppy flowers in his mother's garden… This is different. Secret. It's too big for him. Pain. Struggle. The threat of violence. Darkness and over them the blood-stained sky.

Suddenly he remembers the foxes and he whirls around. Silent, the scrub comes up from the valley below and watches him. He can feel it. Bear. Panther. Tiger. They are all there. He can see their shapes in his mind and the shine of their eyes. Foxes. Only the foxes are real. He knows that. But he knows the others are there too. He knows it because of the pounding of his blood and the sudden dryness of his mouth. His father. His father in the darkness and his mother, her hands held up to her face. 'Don't. Oh please, Jon, don't.' The hunted. Oh! the hunted so defenceless and so…so pitiful.

He bites fiercely at his lip and bends down to pick up a handful of sharp stones. He's armed now. He's crossed over. Hunted still, but he too now, he is a hunter. 'I could…' he whispers. 'If he comes back, my father, I could…' He clutches his stones so hard, they cut into his hand. He's glad of the pain. It makes him strong.

Behind him, the little ewe shudders again and he thinks he hears her moan.

Night now. Above the rim of hills behind the house, the first quivering stars. He sucks in his breath. His mother has forgotten him. He is alone.

Flurry of wind in the grass. A bird. The distant barking of a dog. Over by the fence, the suddenly restless sheep. Then…then…coming down from the house towards him the little bobbing light of his mother's torch. He gives a glad cry and drops his hard-held stones. She has released him. He's a little boy again.

'She all right?' Mum swings the torch so Nadia is caught in an arc of light. She lurches to her feet and they see beside her, miraculous, the little wet bundle.

'Oh, look. Look. I didn't know.'

'We'll wait a bit. Give them time to get to know one another before we put them in the shed.'

The ewe bends over the lamb with soft croonings and it struggles, once, twice, till it disentangles its clumsy legs and stands alone. Jamie reaches out to touch it. Ears, nose, the delicate curve of its throat. It pushes against his hand and in the circle of light he sees for a moment its wide and wondering eyes.

Behind him, he feels the shadows in the scrub cringe and slink away and he lifts his face to the star-studded sky and laughs aloud.

from *Light on Dark Water*

Butterflies

As soon as she's finished her bottle, I take Ruby into the lounge and set her down on the floor with her toys. She reaches for her giraffe and holds it against her cheek. In the last month or so it's become her favourite. Will's pleased. He bought it for her when I first shifted in with him.

Christine's on the other side of the room, reading. She's got her head half turned away but I can see her lips move as she sounds out the words to herself. She's not so clever then.

I go over to her and say, 'I'm just going outside to fetch in the washing before it rains. Ruby'll be all right for a minute. If she does start to cry, you come and get me.'

Christine doesn't answer. I don't expect her to. For just an instant, though, her eyes dart towards the baby. She's got dark eyes, almost black and large enough to be innocent, but you can't tell anything from them, not what she's thinking anyway. They must be like her mother's because Will's eyes are small and grey and crinkled up from laughing too much.

When I come back in, Ruby's screaming. I dump the clothes in the laundry and run and I'm just in time to see Christine scuttle away from her. My heart's beating so fast I can hardly breathe but I snatch Ruby up and whirl to face her. 'What did you do? Come on. Tell me. What did you do to my baby?'

Christine shrugs. She's looking full at me now all right but her face is a mask. Dark eyes under straight black fringe, clear-cut mouth, round little chin. A doll's face and behind it, Christine, the real Christine, the Christine only I know about.

'I didn't do anything,' she says primly, picking up her book. 'She dropped one of her toys. I was just giving it back to her.'

I don't say anything. I take Ruby back into the kitchen and sit down with her in the nearest chair. I start to rock her backwards and forwards in my arms. So familiar, the weight of her, the smell of her, her silky hair against my cheek. At last her eyelids start to flutter. Butterflies, I think, butterflies… Ever since she was born…a tenderness….oh, my baby, my baby…

When she's asleep, I carry her carefully to our room and put her in her cot. Will's not happy with her being in with us, she's not his child, but I won't have her sharing a room with Christine.

Outside the rain's begun again making the colours of the garden blur and run together. I move away from the window and set up the ironing board so I can start on Will's shirts. He's very particular but I don't mind. I like ironing. It's a family thing. And this, well, this is my first proper home. What I had with Mum and Larry doesn't count. That wasn't real. That wasn't me choosing.

I reach for another shirt. The past doesn't matter. I'm free of it. Will and Ruby and me. Perhaps, next year, our own child. A little boy. Will would like that. A son… I start to imagine him. Liam, we could call him Liam and he'd have fine, dark hair like Ruby's and I'd brush it up so it was all soft and bristly and when he woke up he'd hold out his arms to us, laughing… I'm lost in it. I've got him in the pram and Ruby, a little girl now, is clutching the handle with me.

Then, it's too sudden, I'm jerked back. Christine's there, she's got up and she's walking past me to the kitchen, her book's discarded on the floor, it's pages flutter…oh! butterflies, butterflies… My mind whirls with images, too many images, Ruby, the baby, a flock of white butterflies and Christine, always Christine, sly-faced Christine.

I dart forward and grab her. I grab her and drag her back. My breath catches in my throat and I hold, for just a moment I hold her arm against the hot iron. Her eyes go wide and she screams. She's in her eyes all right now. She's frightened. She screams and pulls herself away from me. She's an animal, a little animal whimpering. Behind me I think I hear my mother laugh and I clench my hands against the things I will not let myself remember.

I take a deep breath and I make my voice very quiet and I say, 'You'd better let me look at that, Christine, put some cream on it for you. I've told you before. You mustn't pull at your father's shirt when I'm ironing it. You have to be careful, very careful.' I pause and then I add, 'It's like when you're giving Ruby back her toys. You have to be careful then too. Otherwise…well, otherwise she might cry.'

Christine's retreated to her seat in the corner. She's nursing her arm and rocking herself. 'I didn't…' she begins but then she bites at her lip and ducks her head.

I fetch the lanolin from the bathroom cabinet and tear an old sheet into strips. I sit down next to her and start to bandage her arm. She doesn't say anything but her eyes give her away. She's made her face a mask but she can't quite hide the apprehension in her eyes.

'There,' I say, straightening up and tying the ends of the bandage together so that they look like little white wings. 'There. All fixed. I'll get you a drink and you can go on with your reading while I finish off the ironing.'

She turns her head away quickly but I've seen enough. She knows. I smile to myself and nod. She knows now.

After a while I go back into the bedroom to check on Ruby. She's still asleep.

I kneel down by her cot and put my hand through the bars so I can touch her cheek. So soft. I lift my head. 'No one's going to hurt you, Ruby,' I whisper. 'Not ever. I'm not going to let them.'

Then something breaks inside me and I hear myself cry out. 'No one's going to hurt you, Ruby, not…not like they hurt me.'

Hair Ribbons

It's the end of the war and I am a little girl digging in the dirt. My father's there, he's back now from being a soldier, and Mr McLaughlin, and the old dog Blue that goes everywhere with them like he's their shadow.

My father says, 'You stay here, Possum. I'll just be the other side of the paddock, helping the boss with the fence.'

'All right.'

There's a stone buried in the dirt. I poke at it with my stick till it's loose enough to pick up. It feels ordinary but I know it isn't. It's got shiny bits in it that glitter in the sun. I open my hand to look at it again.

I stretch my legs out in front of me and tilt back my head. Blue sky and a sudden rush of yellow hills. A clump of gum trees. The windmill. The cattle by the dam. Over to the side, Dad and Mr McLaughlin threading new wire through the fence posts. I squint up my eyes till they get blinded with sunlight and I have to look away.

I put the stone carefully into the pocket of my skirt and climb onto the gate so I can go on watching.

****

I'm five, then six years old.

Dad's by the stove cooking flapjacks for tea. 'Things have gotta change, Poss. I don't want them to but that's the way it is.'

I put down the pencil I've been drawing with at the other side of the table. It's a new pencil that Dad's just got for me, a whole box of them, all different colours, red and blue and pink and orange and purple.

'What d'y mean, change?'

'School. Now you're six, you gotta go to school.' He tilts the pan to spread the batter. 'I went and saw the sisters up at St Joseph's. They said they'd have you there. Real nice, they are, those sisters. Your mother never liked them but she was wrong, quite wrong.' He stops suddenly. He didn't mean to say it, that bit about my mother. We never talk about her. She went away a long time ago and I don't really remember. Except the train. I remember that. Her getting on the train and the train leaving and it getting smaller and smaller till the distance finally swallowed it up.

Dad says quickly, 'Sister Peter gave me a uniform for you. 'S a bit big but Mrs Richardson at the shop is going to fix it up. And wait… Look what Mrs Richardson's given me for you.' He slides the cooked flapjack onto a plate and fumbles in his pocket for a twist of brown paper. 'There! What d'y think of that?'

Ribbon. It's a piece of ribbon. I let my fingers slide over it, frowning. It's got a gloss to it like when I colour the sky in hard with my new blue pencil.

'For your hair,' Dad says, nodding. 'Monday morning we'll tie back your hair with it. Wait and see. In your uniform with your hair all tidy you'll be Pamela Helen, a proper little school girl.'

'I don't…' I begin but he won't listen.

''S not us, Possum, not what we want, you and me, but what's gotta be. Can't have you growing up all wild like one of them brumby horses.'

I stir the ribbon round with one finger. 'I'd like to be like that.' I whisper. 'A brumby…'

Dad doesn't hear. He's picked up the frying pan again. 'Nothing for you to worry about, Poss. The sisters'll look after you. They've promised. They've promised to look after you special.'

***

It's hard being Pamela Helen.

I stand under the veranda outside my classroom and watch the other children. The boys shout and jump and run. They're like the firecrackers Dad got me last Guy Fawkes Day.

'Squibs,' I whisper and I smile to myself.

One squib, Roger Neale, has even got red hair. The girls are quieter; they have a shine to them like Mr McLaughlin's horses. They toss their heads and look at me sideways out of wide, long-lashed eyes. Lillian.

Maureen. Wendy. Sheila. I say their names aloud as if they are the words of a song. They stand in a little group under the pepper tree their arms threaded around one another's waists, whispering secrets. They don't talk to me. They pretend I'm not there. I don't care. I don't care at all.

Sometimes, when it's windy or after a squall of rain, I can't help myself. I come down from the veranda. I throw back my head and start to run. Round and round I go, a brumby from the high country. I put my head down and buck and my hair comes free from its ribbon and tumbles down my back.

Suddenly I stop. Dad doesn't want me to be a brumby. He wants me to be like the other girls. Ashamed, I search until I find my lost ribbon. Back on the veranda, I wind it round and round my finger till at last it's time for Maureen to ring the bell.

When school finishes at the end of the day, I don't go home like the others. I stay with Miss Martin till Dad comes for me. Miss Martin isn't a proper teacher – that's Sister Veronica and Sister Peter; she just helps. When the sisters are there she's very quiet and respectful, 'Yes Sister', 'No, Sister', but when it's only me, she's different. It's like we're friends. Lillian and Maureen and Wendy and now, now Pamela Helen and Miss Martin. We go outside and play hopscotch together. Other times, when it's raining, we stay in the classroom and she writes words on the blackboard for me. I trace the shapes of the letters with my fingers and try to remember what they say. Dog. Cat. Boy. Girl. Father. Mother. My hand stops then and skitters away as if it's frightened.

Miss Martin doesn't notice. 'What else, Pamela Helen? You choose. Quick, before your dad gets here.'

'Horse. Write horse.'

She does it in red and, as soon as she's finished, I close my eyes so I can see them, Mr McLaughlin's horses, running towards me, all slender legs and tossing manes and soft dark eyes. I hold out my hand and one of them, the golden one with the foal, thrusts out her muzzle and blows against my fingers.

Miss Martin gives me a piece of brown chalk and we both draw horses all over the blackboard.

***

130

I'm eleven, then twelve years old.

'Growing up, Poss,' says Dad, smiling.

I nod but I don't say anything. I can feel it happening but I'm not sure I like it. Everything's changing. All the familiar things. Autumn with the spiderwebs along the fences, the dark wet earth, the first bright shoots of grass and then winter, shredded clouds above the hills, wind and hail. Spring, the buds on the willow fronds along the creek, Mrs Richardson's poppies, gold and cream and dawn-pink, a white plum tree. It hurts inside me. I don't understand that, spring hurting. It's like…it's like I'm standing on tip-toe…reaching…reaching…

At home by myself I wander from room to room touching things. The clock. The china dogs my great-grandparents brought from England. The green painted kitchen chairs. The hat stand. My father's highland jug that plays a tune when you pick it up. It's like I'm seeing them for the first time. 'Pamela Helen,' I whisper. 'Pamela Helen,' and even my name sounds as if it belongs to someone else, someone new, someone I don't know yet.

Then at the beginning of summer, the letter. Dad brings it into my room where I'm sprawled on the floor outlining a map of Australia.

'Poss, look at this.'

I put down my pencil and stare up at him.

'Your mother…' The words jam in his throat so he has to begin again. 'Your mother. She wants to see you. She's coming this way to stay with her cousin Rosemary and on the way back she wants…'

'But…but why?'

He shakes his head and turns the letter over. 'She doesn't say. Just… where is it…just…"I would like to call in and see Pamela Helen. Surely after all this time you can't object to that…".'

It's very quiet. Outside a dog barking, the wind, a car on the gravelled road behind the house. The clock ticking.

'Can't you say you do object? That…' My voice drops to a whisper. 'I don't want to see her. I…'

'Oh, Possum. That wouldn't be right. She's your mother. She…'

'She left me.'

It's torn from me, a cry, a wild bird's cry, but my father leans forward and puts out his hand to touch my cheek and restores me to myself.

'We have to do what's right, Possum. There's no other way.'

'I guess so.'

He fumbles with the letter again. 'I'm to pick her up at the station at two-thirty and then take her back in time to catch the next train.'

I take a deep breath. 'Scones,' I say. 'And jam cockles. Mrs Richardson's showed me how to make both those and a layer cake.'

Dad nods and goes to the door. 'That's my girl. That's my best girl.'

I close my homework book and get up to go over to the window. Outside the vegetable garden, the apricot tree, a sprawl of passionfruit vine over the galvanised roof of the chook shed. Everything the same and everything different.

***

I take the scones out of the oven and wrap them in a clean tea towel. I've got everything ready in the front room, plates, jug, sugar bowl, the sliced layer cake and the biscuits, all carefully set out on the starched lace tablecloth. As soon as Dad comes back from the railway station with my mother, I'll boil the kettle and butter the scones…

I go into my room to re-plait my hair. My face looks back at me from the mirror, wide-eyed, freckled, a child's face staring… I bite at my lip and start on my plaits. When I've finished, I loop them together and tie them with red ribbons. It's a good colour, red, better than blue or pink. It's a bugle-sounding colour.

They're at the front door. I hear my father say, 'Go on in, Elsie, through to the lounge. I'll get Pamela Helen,' and I make myself go out into the hallway to meet them.

Everyone I know, Dad, me, Mrs Richardson, her little girl Pauline, even the sisters at school, we're all the same, ordinary, sparrows, just sparrows. My mother's different, a picture I saw once in a book, a sun bird.

My chest is so tight I can hardly breathe. 'Mother.'

She takes a step or two toward me and then she turns back to my father and stops. 'Oh, Stan. This can't be Pamela Helen. Why, why she's all grown up.'

'I'm twelve.'

'But…but…' Suddenly her fluttering hands take on purpose and she pushes forward a little boy. 'This is Johnnie. Johnnie, say hello to Pamela Helen.'

He's not much more than a baby, two, three, round-cheeked; he's got a tumble of very fair hair and underneath it, eyes dark enough to be my own.

'Johnnie?'

'Yes. Your brother.' She turns again to my father. 'I adopted him. I had to. I was so lonely.' Her lips quiver but her eyes, carefully watching, don't change. 'You have no idea how lonely it gets in the city on your own.'

My father nods. 'It's all right, Elsie. I understand. Come into the lounge. Pamela Helen will bring us in a cup of tea.'

The tight feeling in my chest is worse. Red ribbons, oh, red ribbons. I clench my hands and go into the kitchen to light the gas jets under the kettle. I shut my eyes and pretend Sister Peter's with me. I let her voice steady me. Boil the kettle. Butter the scones. Warm the teapot. Put in the tea leaves, a spoonful for each person and one for the pot. I stop. The little boy. Johnnie. He can't drink tea. I climb onto a chair to get my old rabbit beaker from the back of the cupboard. I put it on the tray next to the plate of scones and half fill it with milk. Mrs Richardson always does that for Pauline, half fills her cup with milk so she won't spill any…

I carry the tray into the lounge room. Put it on the table. Smile. Ask your mother how she likes her tea. I feel better. It's working. Inside myself I watch Sister Peter nod at me and I pour the tea for them both and hand them their cups.

'Well,' says my mother, accepting a buttered scone and placing it daintily on her plate. 'Well, Stan, you've certainly gone to a lot of trouble.'

'It wasn't me. It was Pamela Helen.'

'Really? All of this? Pamela Helen?' She regards me over the rim of her cup. 'Well, I am impressed.'

'I…I just wanted…' I stop, confused, but it's all right, she's going on as if I haven't said anything.

'And it's no use me pretending and asking you for the recipes because, your father knows, I've never been much good at, you know, cooking or…' She's laughing now, her eyes all crinkled up at the corners and my father's smiling and though I don't want to, I have to smile too.

'You know what, Stan?' she says suddenly, interrupting herself. 'Pamela Helen's just like your mother.'

'I don't…'

'Yes. You must see it. The way she's managed everything and, I never noticed before but she was only little then, she looks like her too. See. Her mouth. The line of her jaw. That's your mother. It is, Stan. It is.'

'I've…I've got a grandmother…?'

'No, Possum. Not now. She…'

'She died,' says my mother before he can finish. 'Just before you were born. I was sorry about that. She never liked me of course, too flighty, she said but I was sorry she died when she did, she was so looking forward to the baby.' She puts down her cup and smoothes her skirt over her knees. 'Your father wanted me to name you after her. Amelia Alice. I couldn't do that though. So old-fashioned.' Her face changes again and her eyes dart toward my father. 'Maybe I should have. Maybe it would have been more appropriate seeing as how she takes after her and not me.'

I duck my head and watch my hands twist themselves together in my lap. 'I'm sorry.' I whisper. 'I don't mean to…'

'Doesn't matter. Doesn't matter at all.'

It does, though. I know it does. I lean forward. 'Mother, I…'

She's not listening. She's turned away from me to the little boy. 'You all right, Johnnie? Want some more of your milk? We'll be going soon, back on the train. You'll like that, won't you? We'll make you a bit of a bed on the seat next to me and you can have a little sleep with the teddy Auntie Rosemary made you.' She's someone else now. Her voice. Her hands. The softness in her face. She's…she's his mother.

Something cries out inside of me. All these years. I've been waiting all these years and I never knew. Her voice. Her hands. Oh, Mother, Mother…

Desperate, I turn to Dad. He's sitting hunched forward, his arms hanging down between his thighs, his face old and grey and bleak.

I want to run to him. I want to say…

But…but…there is nothing to say. She doesn't want us. She doesn't want either of us.

I take a deep breath. Ribbons, oh, my red, red ribbons. I lift my head. I do it for my father. I do it for both of us so she won't know how much we mind. 'Another cup of tea, Mother, before you go. And Johnnie, perhaps you'd like one of my special biscuits.'

I know what it feels like now to be grown up.

Baby Crying

The summer I'm six is different. I'm not sure why. Perhaps it's because I know I have to go to school soon. I stand by the window watching the sparrows playing on the lawn underneath the sprinkler.

'Once you're at school, you'll find out,' says my mother. 'You'll find out what's what then.'

Before she can say anything else, Charlotte interrupts her. 'Oh, don't tell her that, Deirdre. You'll scare her.'

I turn round but I don't say anything. My mother gets angry if I say too much. It's different for Charlotte. She can say what she likes. She isn't afraid of Mum. She doesn't have to be. Mum isn't her mother. Her mother married my father a long time ago but then she went away and married someone else. Sometimes Charlotte goes and stays with them. I don't like that. I lift my chin. Charlotte's my sister. She belongs with me.

Mum's mouth goes tight. 'She might as well know,' she says. 'School'll be a shock to her. She's spoilt here.'

'Oh, Deirdre, I don't think…'

Mum gets up from her chair and goes over to the mantelpiece. She picks up one of the ivory elephants my father brought back from India. Her voice changes. 'School ruins your children,' she says as if she's suddenly got very tired. 'Everyone knows that. It takes them away from you. Wait and see. It'll change Zayley too. It'll make her rude and full of herself.'

My mouth's so dry I can hardly speak. 'Couldn't I…couldn't I stay home and…' I swallow and have to begin again. 'Couldn't you and Charlotte teach me and then…'

'Don't be ridiculous.' Mum's lip curls and her eyes start to glitter dangerously. 'How could I teach you? You never listen to me.'

'Charlotte…'

'Charlotte's got her studies at the university.'

'Then…then maybe we could pretend…' My voice is no more than a whisper. I can hardly hear it. 'Please, Mummy. Please. I don't want to go to school. I don't want…'

My mother laughs then. She puts the elephant on the shelf with the others and throws back her head and laughs. I don't like the sound of it. My hands clench at my sides. Glass, I think, it sounds like glass breaking and I hold myself very still and stare down at the carpet. It isn't an ordinary carpet. My father got it in India when he got the elephants. But it's spoiled now. Instead of flowers I can only see the scattered fragments of my mother's laughter. Frightened, I turn and run outside.

***

It's too hot to sleep. I kick out restlessly with my legs. In the room next to mine, I can hear my mother and father. I go suddenly very still. Something's wrong. I can hear it in their voices. My father's voice is low and hesitant but my mother cries out as if something's hurt her. Bambi's mother, I think, squeezing my eyes shut, Bambi's mother alone in the forest…

I get up very quietly and creep to their door. It's almost shut but a little bit of light spills out through the gap. It's like a blade. It cuts the shadows in half. My heart starts to feel too big for my chest and I have to put my hands up to hold it in.

I hear my mother again. 'No. I told you before. I told you when I agreed to Zayley and you promised. I won't have it. I won't.' Her voice drops and breaks. 'Oh, Jack, Jack, don't you understand. I won't have another one. I can't.'

I start to shiver then. She sounds like a little girl. She sounds like me. I wrap my arms around myself and wait for her to say something else but she doesn't, neither of them do, so in the end I have to go back to bed.

***

I'm sitting on my bedroom floor making patterns with my paper clips. Charlotte gave me a new box of coloured ones for Christmas. I sit back on my heels frowning.

Charlotte interrupts me. She looks rushed. She sits down on my bed and then she says carefully, 'Your mother…I thought I'd better tell you, Zayley. Your mother has to go to hospital for a few days.'

All at once my chest is too tight. 'She's sick? Mum's sick?'

'Not…not exactly. Just…' Her hands twist in her lap. 'She's going to be all right. You…you don't have to worry. It's only for a day or two and then she'll be home again. Only…only when she comes home, you'll have to be very quiet, you'll have to make sure …'

I nod. I lean forward to place an orange paper clip next to a red one. A rainbow, I think suddenly, I can make a rainbow… Red and orange and yellow and blue… Charlotte's still watching. Her mouth's quivering. There's something she's not telling me.

I smile to reassure her. 'You don't have to worry,' I say. 'I'll be quiet. I promise.' Quiet's easy. I'm good at being quiet.

Charlotte gets up then. She comes over and kneels next to me. 'I know,' she says, brushing the hair out of my eyes. 'I know. You're not any trouble, Zayley. You never have been. I just…I just don't understand Deirdre. I don't understand how she can…' She breaks off. She's been talking to herself.

I don't mind. Words aren't important. They get in the way. It's feelings that count. Whenever I'm with Charlotte, I get a good feeling. I feel safe.

Charlotte stirs her finger round my box of paper clips. 'Purple,' she says. 'You need purple.' Then her eyes meet mine and she smiles.

Charlotte's my sister. I let her put the purple one in place to complete the rainbow.

***

Summer's almost over. I start school. It's not nearly as bad as my mother said. The teacher writes words on the blackboard for us to copy. I like the shape of them. I like the pictures they make in my mind. Friday afternoon's best though. We have painting then. I paint birds and trees and flowers. Once, shuddering, I paint Bambi's mother in the forest. The teacher says it's very good but I know better so the next week I paint something else.

Charlotte comes home from a visit to her mother and we all have breakfast together. Everyone's very quiet. I look from one to the other. My father's frowning over his newspaper. Charlotte, pink-cheeked, is humming to herself as she spreads marmalade on her toast. She's got a secret. She showed me his photograph and made me promise not to tell. I smile, remembering. My mother is staring out into the garden. Her eyes are wide and very dark. It's not like her. She's too still.

I stir my cornflakes with my spoon and my mother says sharply, 'Stop that. Stop that at once, Zayley. Stop playing with your food.' Her words have broken a spell. She tears at her croissant with thin, impatient fingers and I hear my father sigh.

Outside in the garden the honeyeaters are busy in the bottle-brush. I watch the flash of their wings in the light. Next week, when I go back to school, I'll paint them; it'll be better than Bambi's mother and the teacher will say…

Suddenly I put down my spoon. There's a baby crying. A baby crying in the garden. I can't see it through the window but I can hear it. Little, whimpering cries.

I push back my chair and stand up. 'There's a baby,' I tell them. 'Somewhere in the garden there's a baby. I can hear it crying.'

No one takes any notice. It's like they can't hear me. I run to my mother and pull at her arm. 'There's a baby,' I say, suddenly desperate. 'Can't you hear it? A baby crying in the garden.'

My mother tries to laugh. Her hands twist themselves together and fly to her mouth. 'Whatever are you talking about, Zayley? How can there be a baby in the garden?'

'There is. There must be. I can hear it crying.'

Charlotte says quickly, too quickly, 'A kitten, Zayley. You can hear a kitten. Mrs Stevens next door, she's got…'

My mother puts both her hands on the table and forces herself to her feet. She looks too tall. It's like she fills all the space in the room. 'Go and look then,' she says. Her lips start to quiver but she jerks her head up and shouts, 'Charlotte, take her outside and let her look. So stupid. There's no baby. I tell you, there's no baby in the garden or anywhere else.'

Behind her, in the garden, I hear the baby wail again and I run to Charlotte and grab her hand. 'There is a baby,' I say again. 'I know there is. I can hear it. A little lost baby crying for its mother.'

My mother lunges toward me, both her hands outstretched and my father gets up quickly and puts his arm around her.

'You heard, Charlotte,' he hisses. 'Take your sister outside and don't bring her back till I tell you.'

We spend all morning looking for the baby but we don't find it.

'I told you,' says Charlotte flinging herself down, breathless, into the shade of the ash tree. 'I told you, Zayley. It was Mrs Stevens's kitten.' She won't look at me, though. She plucks at the grass instead. Her hands are like my mother's. For the first time, I see her hands are like my mother's.

Sighing, I turn away. The garden's very quiet. I rest my chin on my knees and watch a butterfly dancing by itself in a sudden shaft of sunlight.

Blue Plate

Julia stops in front of the tool shed. 'We ought to climb up there,' she says. 'We'd be able to see heaps from the roof. Spy on people and all.'

Ellie's doubtful. 'There's nothing to see. Just our place and Weston's vineyards. You can't even see their house because of all the trees.' She pauses, frowning. 'And even if we did see old Mr Weston, so what?'

Julia doesn't answer. She screws up her eyes. 'Look, all we have to do is climb on the drum there, reach for that branch and swing ourselves over. I'll go first if you're scared.'

'I'm not, it's just that Grandpa…'

'Oh, come on, Ellie. It'll be fun. Besides, you said your grandfather had gone away for a few days. You said he'd gone to Melbourne to see your Aunt Alice.'

'He has. But Mum, there's still Mum and…'

'She's inside. She won't know and if she finds out, I'll think of something. She likes me. It'll be all right. Come on.'

But Ellie's still hesitant. 'My mother doesn't like you, Julia,' she says slowly. 'She only pretends because… Well, I'm not sure why 'cept you live near us and your mother's on the hospital committee with her.'

Julia's suddenly very still. Her pale eyes narrow. 'What are you going on about? Of course she likes me. Last week she bought me hair ribbons just like yours so we'd look like twins and she always lets me sleep over even on school nights and…'

Ellie purses up her mouth. 'That doesn't mean anything. Yesterday, when I came in from collecting the eggs, I heard her tell Mrs Worthington you were spoilt. She said she was tired of the way your mother took advantage of us, always expecting her to look after you.'

Julia's cheeks go pink and her head jerks up. 'She has no right to say things like that about me. Or about Mother. And she's not getting away with it either. I'm going to tell her so too. Just you watch. I'm going to go up to her right now. Mrs Mitchell, I'll say, how dare you…'

'Wait,' says Ellie, suddenly frightened. 'You can't do that. You can't say anything to Mum. She'll know I told and…'

'Why shouldn't you tell me? She shouldn't have said it.'

'But…but… Oh, Julia, please, you can't. I'll get into trouble. She…'

'She won't do anything to you. She won't dare. Not after I've finished with her.'

Ellie drops her head. Her lips quiver. 'My mother,' she whispers. 'My mother when she's angry, she…' She can't go on. She scuffs at the grass with the toe of her sneaker. 'Julia, you're my friend, aren't you? My best friend. Please, please don't say anything to Mum.' Then, remembering something, she flings back her head and cries desperately, 'Julia, Julia, if you don't say anything, I'll give you, I'll give you my blue plate.'

There's a little silence then. Julia smoothes down her skirt. 'Well, I'll think about it.' Her eyes flick toward Ellie. 'What plate? You never told me you had a plate.'

Ellie's words fall over one another. 'Grandpa gave it to me last week. You'll like it. I know you will. You can put it on your dressing table. It's got birds on it and curly flowers and… Wait a minute, I'll get it for you.' She turns and darts back down the path without even waiting to see if Julia's following. She's got a wooden box under the ash tree where she keeps her treasures. 'Here it is. Oh, Julia, you do like it, don't you? It's cracked a bit but you can hardly see, not if you hold it right and…'

But Julia won't commit herself. 'Where did your grandfather get it?' she asks. 'It looks sort of ordinary to me.'

'Oh, he's always buying boxes of old crockery at those sales he goes to. You know that. He plants things in them. In the cups and jugs and teapots, I mean. Plates aren't much good, though. That's why he gave it to me. He thought I'd like it.'

Julia nods. Her eyes are suddenly very bright and she reaches over and takes the plate from Ellie. 'And you do like it, don't you Ellie?' she says softly. 'You like it a lot.'

For a moment Ellie can't answer. She looks at the ground. 'Yes,' she whispers at last. 'Yes. It's my best thing.'

Julia's face goes very still. 'I think perhaps we won't climb onto the tool shed roof today. We'll make cakes instead.'

'Cakes? But Mum…'

'Not real ones, stupid. Pretend.' She looks around her. 'Over there. Near the olive trees. The dirt's good there. Sort of crumbly.'

'Oh! Mud pies! You mean mud pies.'

'Cakes.' Julia draws herself up to her full height and looks dignified. 'Mud pies are for little children.'

Ellie nods and runs to fetch a bucket of water. She squats next to Julia and watches as her small deft hands shape the wet dirt into triangles and crescents and little lopsided stars. They decorate them with red boxthorn berries and marigold petals and sprigs of rosemary.

'Worthy of my plate,' says Julia, smiling.

Ellie looks at her quickly but she doesn't say anything more, so Ellie bends her head over the cakes again. She doesn't like Julia's smile. It doesn't reach her eyes, she thinks and… Sly, remembers Ellie all at once. Mum said that too. A sly little puss and Ellie shivers even though they're sitting in the sun; she shivers and her hands, busy with the marigolds, falter so she drops most of them on the ground.

***

Days pass. Julia walks home from school with Ellie every afternoon. She hesitates at the gate till Ellie asks her in. Once she even goes up to Ellie's mother. 'It's so nice of you to let me play with Ellie, Mrs Mitchell,' she says boldly. 'I hope I'm not making a nuisance of myself.'

Ellie catches her breath. For a moment she can't breathe but Julia's face is quite innocent and Mum, Mum just shrugs and goes on ironing one of Grandpa's shirts.

Friday's different. Ellie's got her piano lesson.

'I'll go to your place and wait for you under the ash tree if you like,' says Julia. 'Then we can play for a while when you get home. Your mum won't mind, will she?'

'Course not. You can look at my treasures.'

When Ellie gets home, though, Julia's not there. She stands under the ash tree for a moment, frowning. The stillness, there's something about the stillness… She lifts her head. The colour is beginning to go from the sky and the shadows, the shadows across the lawn seem suddenly far too dark Dropping her bag, Ellie turns and runs toward the house. 'Mum. Mum.' She wrenches open the kitchen door and stumbles inside. 'Mum, have you seen Julia because…' She stops then and backs away because she's seen her mother's face. It's too late, though. Her mother's mouth twists and she grabs Ellie by the shoulder. 'Julia,' she hisses. 'You don't need to bother about Julia. You won't be seeing her again.'

'Mum…'

'Don't start. Don't you dare start, Elinor. My own daughter. To think, my own daughter.'

Ellie sees then that she's got Grandpa's belt in her hand. It twitches like something alive, like the snake Grandpa killed last summer when he found it sunning itself by the water trough. Ellie screams and tries to pull away but her mother's too strong for her and the belt comes down again and again across her bare legs.

At last Mum's satisfied. 'Get to your room,' she says, panting. 'I've had just about enough of you. Always making trouble. Always sneaking around listening. You repeat anything I say again and you'll be sorry. You remember that, Miss. You make sure you remember that.'

Ellie doesn't answer. She can't. Her legs hurt. But it's not that. She's used to that. It's something else. Something worse. She grabs hold of the door frame to steady herself and closes her eyes. Images explode in her mind. Red berries and marigold petals, the gleam of water, Julia's hands. Julia. Julia looking up at her smiling, her smile so seemingly sweet and her wide eyes… Julia, her friend. Julia, who has betrayed her.

Moaning, Ellie moves her head from side to side. 'Oh, my plate,' she whispers, her clenched fist in her mouth. 'Oh, my plate, my pretty blue plate.'

Angus

When I wake up, everything looks different. The faded blue rug on the floor. The lampshade. The chair by the door. The broken bamboo blind across the window. I sit up and push the hair out of my eyes. It's the light, it's the light that has changed. All those other mornings when I woke up, the room was full of dancing light and now…

In the room next to mine, Angus is talking to his lion, the lion I bought him last Saturday. I get up quickly and go to the window but I don't pull back the blind. Outside I can hear the sea. I shut my eyes and I'm a little girl again running through the dunes to the beach. The wind tangles my hair, it whips sand against my bare legs and shudders for a moment in the sparse dry grasses but I am running toward the sea oh! magic of sun on water, the wide expanse of the sky, the wheeling silver gulls… My breath catches in my throat. It was so simple then. Mum. Dad. My brother Paul. Summer holidays at the shack. I didn't know then what was ahead of me.

Angus is calling me. 'Mamma. Mamma.'

I don't answer him. I can't. I know now why the light has changed. It's because I have to give him back. It's Saturday again and I have to give him back.

After he's finished his breakfast, I dress Angus in his new dungarees and shirt and buckle on his sandals. He looks…'cared for,' I whisper defiantly and I stand him in front of the mirror so he can watch me comb his hair. For a moment I see our faces reflected together, mother and child, and I bite at my lip and turn my head quickly away.

'Come,' I say, extending my hand. 'Come, Angus, we're not going down to the beach today. We have to go out in the car.'

His eyes go round and solemn. 'Car,' he repeats. 'Car,' and then he smiles.

I make myself smile back though it's a lot harder than I expect.

Expect. The word quivers in my mind like something alive. I never expected any of this.

***

Last Saturday afternoon. If I close my eyes, I can see it, pictures in my mind, a loop of film. I'm in my garden setting out the petunia seedlings. Round the side of the house the honeyeaters are squabbling in the gum blossom. I straighten up, smiling. I planted those trees myself when I bought the house eight years ago. I go round to watch them. It's like being in church. Sky, birds, the flamboyant scarlet flowers, a stained-glass window, and inside myself a sudden quietness. More than that. I press my hands against my throat. Ever since Richard left me, I've relied on the birds. I can't explain it. They are all I have left.

After a while I go back to my planting. I bend down to pick up my trowel and then I stop. There's a child in my driveway, a little boy, all he's got on is in an old T-shirt several sizes too large and he's squatting down pouring gravel from one hand to the other. He looks up. Under a fall of thick fair hair, his eyes are unexpectedly dark, almost black. I catch my breath and then I start to shudder. It's like I recognise him.

I go right up to him and hold out my hand. 'Come with me,' I say. 'Come with me and I'll get you a drink.'

He feels it too. He drops his stones and puts his hand in mine and we go into the kitchen together.

***

I always intended to have children. But there were so many other things. My father's dependence on me after my mother's death. My career. My late marriage. Richard himself… In the end it didn't seem to matter.

Except….except… That last confrontation when Richard told me he was leaving me. A trophy wife, I thought, Fiona will only be a trophy wife and I half-turned to the window so I could distract myself by watching the sparrows on the lawn. A trophy wife meant nothing to me. I had had time to grow into myself, gain serenity, grace, composure. What was a

145

pretty face to that, even a young, pretty face? Richard would soon tire of her and when he did, he'd come back to me. I smoothed down my skirt and smiled to myself. Richard got up and went over to the sideboard to pour himself another drink. His voice changed. 'A son,' he whispered. 'I always wanted a son and now, well now…' He squared his shoulders and I couldn't hide any more from the truth. He wasn't leaving me because Fiona was young and pretty. He was leaving me because she was pregnant with his child and I…I had left it too late.

When I turned back to the window, the sparrows had gone. The shadows of the trees lay across the lawn in dark irregular stripes but the birds themselves had flown away.

***

So on Saturday I take the little boy into my kitchen and sit him at the table with a plastic tumbler of orange juice. 'Here you are,' I tell him. 'You drink this while I get ready.'

Once in my bedroom, I pull down a suitcase and fill it with clothes. My hands are deft, folding slips and bras and briefs, they reach for sweaters and skirts and the blouses I usually wear to work. I want to laugh at them, my hands; they are so at odds with the tumult of emotions inside me. I catch sight of my face in the wardrobe mirror and stop suddenly. I don't look like myself. I put my hand up and trace very gently the contours of my face. Eyes. Cheeks. Lips. She looks so young, this other Evelyn, a girl realising a dream. I remember the sparrows on the lawn and how I felt when I saw they'd flown away and I start to shudder again. I have to put my arms around myself to hold myself still. She doesn't know enough, this other Evelyn, she doesn't know… Treachery…the treachery of a man who said he didn't want children and then…

I make myself look into her eyes. 'It's all right,' I tell her. 'You don't have to worry. You've got something now, something of your own at last.'

Quickly I turn and slam down the lid of the case. 'The keys,' I whisper. 'The keys to the shack,' and, picking up the case, I run back to the kitchen where I keep them next to my car keys on a little polished wooden rack by the door.

It's years since I've stayed at the beach shack. Richard never liked it there. 'Too out of the way,' he said, pursing up his mouth. 'You can't even go swimming. The water's too rough.' I didn't say anything. I knew he was right. It was a long time since I'd been a little girl scrambling across the rocks with Paul. Paul. It's because of Paul I've got the keys. 'Dad left the shack to both of us,' he said. 'It's only fair you have keys as well.'

I retrieve the keys and press them against my mouth before I turn to check on the little boy. He's finished his drink. I watch him put the glass carefully back on the table and climb down from his chair.

'Mamma?' he asks. 'Mamma?'

'No,' I say. 'Not yet. We're going to the beach. You and I. First though we'll have to stop at the shops. Get some groceries, some proper clothes for you. A bucket. You'll need that at the beach, won't you? A bucket and spade.'

He tilts his head back so he can look into my face and then he nods. 'Beach,' he repeats. 'Spade.'

Before I can stop myself, I kneel down in front of him and my hand goes out and touches his hair, traces the curve of his cheek. 'Angus,' I whisper. 'Angus.' I straighten up. It's not his name. I know that but, 'Come on, Angus,' says the other Evelyn. 'Come and get in the car. We'll have to hurry if we want to get there before dark.'

***

Time stops. Or maybe it starts. I don't know. Time out of mind. I read that somewhere once but I didn't know what it meant. Now I do. This is time out of mind.

Early morning and the tide coming in. Angus holds my hand. The water, laced with foam, swirls around our bare feet and we laugh aloud. A piece of sea-glass. A cuttlefish. A handful of broken shells. Angus's treasures. He carries them importantly in his bucket and when we get back to the shack, he sits on the floor and arranges them in endless patterns.

Monday, a sudden summer storm. The sea's angry now and Angus, frightened, clutches at my skirt. In the afternoon I find a piece of red seaweed, delicate as a spring flower, and we take it home too and put it in a glass of salt water on the table.

Every day something different. Bleached driftwood. A scuttling crab.

A rock-pool with a school of little darting fish. Seagulls. We throw them the crusts of our sandwiches and they crowd around us, squabbling. Far out to sea an ocean liner, sharply silhouetted against the pale sky. The first stars.

'Look, Angus, look. Wish on a star and it'll come true.'

Sunrise, pink and gold, and at the other side of the cove where the cliffs jut into the sea, a spume of spindrift, white as mermaids' hair. Angus digging with his spade, a shower of sand and behind it his solemn, dreaming face. The sea at evening, grey now the light's going, grey and mysterious, tender even, the sea our mother. Didn't I read that somewhere too, the sea our mother from whence we came, no, no I've made it up but it ought to be true, not mother earth, mother sea…

A shark's egg. Angus turns it around in his hands, frowning. It looks like a rose, a black sea-rose, I think, and then I laugh. I'm always laughing. I'm as young as Angus. I grab his hand and run with him across the damp sand. We are children together. Time out of mind. Nothing matters. We are children together.

***

We go into the nearest town for more groceries, suntan lotion, a red plastic ball. At the last moment I dart into the craft shop and buy a book of patterns and some soft blue wool. Summer now but soon enough autumn and the cold wind off the sea… In the early afternoons while Angus is inside having his nap, I sit on the little front veranda and knit a jumper for my son. Knit one. Purl one. Knit one below. Fisherman's rib. I wind the wool round the needles and smile to myself. I am content to be the other Evelyn, my hair tied back like a schoolgirl, my nose peeling with sunburn, my skirt wrinkled and stained around the hem with sea water.

The gulls in the bay rise shrieking from a fisherman's boat. I pause to consult my pattern. Fiona has her children. I've seen her with them at the supermarket, two little boys with thin faces and cottony fly-away hair. It doesn't matter anymore. It doesn't matter what she and Richard have. I have a son too.

The fishermen have beached their boat but the gulls still wheel above it in eager, ever-widening circles.

Angus wakes in the night, crying. I'm at his side before I'm even aware of it.

'Mamma, Mamma,' he whimpers.

He doesn't mean me, though. Frightened, I stop. Her. He means her. I can see her in his wide, unfocused eyes, his damp hair, his little reaching arms. All week I have not let myself think about her but now, now… She is in the room with us, her eyes dark with accusations.

I lift my head defiantly. 'You didn't look after him properly.' I say. 'He's Angus now,' and before she can answer, I bend down and lift him up. 'Hush, baby, hush. I'm here. A bad dream. You've been having a bad dream. Don't cry. I'm here. Mamma's here.' I sit on his bed and start to rock him. Inside me, something, the other Evelyn, something, cries out exulting, 'See, I'm his mother now. He's forgotten you. He has. He has.'

When the dawn comes, it's like I'm seeing him for the first time. His little half open mouth, his lashes dark against the curve of his cheek, his thick, tumbled hair. There's a bloom on him, his skin's so delicate. Pure, I think and it frightens me.

'It cannot last,' I whisper. 'It cannot ever last.'

I start to lay him down again. One of his hands is clutching the lace of my nightgown and very gently I free myself from it.

And now, morning…morning and the light has changed and I know. I know I have to give him back. Wanting him can't make him mine. The other mother. I'm a mother too now so I know about her. She's in the room with me like she was last night but it's more than that. She's been with me all week, though I wouldn't let myself acknowledge her. She's part of me, part of the other Evelyn, both of us mothers. Angus has tied us together and I have to give him back.

I park the car in a side street next to the police station. In the back seat,

Angus is singing to himself but I don't turn to look at him. Instead I watch my own hands fall away from the steering wheel. They search for one another in my lap and then are very still. I was always so proud of my hands. They were so long and slender and elegant. Evelyn Cooper, deputy principal of Trinity House Girls' College. They were her hands but now…they're uncertain, the hands of the other Evelyn. 'I'm sorry,' I tell her. 'But you knew…you knew all along…'

I lift my head, suddenly resolute. All I have to do is tell them the truth. It should be easy enough. I've dealt with facts all my life. 'I was watching the birds,' I'll say, rehearsing the words aloud. 'I was watching the birds in my red flowering gums and when I came round the side of the house, I saw him playing in my driveway.' My mouth quivers and my hands clutch at one another for reassurance but my voice is very steady. 'I kept him for a while but now, well, now it's time for me to give him back.'

It won't matter. It won't matter what they do to me. All this week I have been a mother and no one can ever take that from me.

The Plum Tree

The day before her wedding, Sinead goes outside and says goodbye to all the trees. It's evening. Shadows are already creeping across the overgrown lawn and Sinead smiles when she sees them. It's a long time since she's let herself play with shadows.

She goes first to the lilly pilly by the front gate. With one finger she traces the outline of a glossy leaf. 'You always waited for me to come home from school,' she says tenderly and she sees herself suddenly, a little schoolgirl, her hair in two tight pigtails tied with scarlet ribbon. She sighs and walks past the tangle of lilac and daphne and African daisy. In the side garden, next to the flagpole, there's a Norfolk pine and a dilapidated palm but she has never loved them so she doesn't stop. They are both too tall. She doesn't think they have ever noticed her.

She pauses by the ash tree, though, and puts a hand out to stroke its trunk. She remembers the endless patterns of light and shade its leaves made on the bare ground every summer. 'Lace,' she says. 'They were like lace,' and her breath catches in her throat. Her sister was always climbing the ash tree. She was as strong as a boy with sturdy, tanned legs and a resolute face. 'Come on, Sinead,' she'd urged. 'It's great up here. We can pretend we're in a ship. Jump up and grab that branch and I'll pull you up.' But Sinead was small and timid. She'd shaken her head and sat down by the trunk instead, making pictures out of marigold petals and bark. The tree didn't mind. It understood.

Sinead sighs and goes round the back of the house to the gum tree. It looks like a street tree. They'd lopped it when she was ten. She bites her lip, remembering. She'd acted like her sister then all right. She'd shouted and stamped her foot and picked up an empty coffee mug and hurled it across the room. 'How dare you!' she'd screamed. 'How dare you! It's my tree, mine, and now you've amputated out its heart.' They'd all stared at her in astonishment and then her grandfather said mildly, 'But, sweetheart, it had to be done. It was dangerous.' She remembered *Seven Little Australians* and the gum tree falling on Judy and she'd started to cry. She didn't want to live in a world where things had to be done. She wanted the world of dreams instead.

After a while she comes to the plum tree. She comes to it slowly, her head bowed, because approaching it is like going up to the altar in church. She loves the plum tree best. It's old and twisted, deformed even, and everyone else has forgotten it. 'Except me,' she whispers. 'Oh, except me,' and she pushes the hair out of her eyes and stands there, just looking at it. Its leaves tremble in the wind and she knows it recognises her. 'Every spring since I was very little, I've come to look at you and marvel. You're old and…and ugly but in the spring you're a bride.' She remembers suddenly that in the morning she too is to be a bride and her lips quiver. 'I'll miss you, oh, I'll miss you. This coming spring I won't be here to see you. No one will. Since Grandpa died, everything's got more and more neglected and now…now they're talking of selling and getting a smaller place in town and who knows what will happen then. Who knows what will happen to either of us because tomorrow…' She stops and puts out a hand to steady herself. 'Trees aren't like people,' she says at last. 'They don't have any choice. They have…they have fortitude instead.' For a moment that comforts her. 'Perhaps it'll be all right. Perhaps someone will buy the house and look after the garden.'

She lifts her face with its suddenly shining eyes and smiles at the plum tree. 'Perhaps someone will buy you who will love you just as much as I have.' She puts her arms around its twisted trunk and leans her cheek against it. 'I never wanted to grow up. I can't tell anyone but you because…' She shuts her eyes so she can see herself one last time, a little girl with the wooden hobby horse her grandfather made her. 'I was safe then,' she whispers. 'I didn't know about people then, how cruel they are, even the children. 'She sighs. 'Especially the children.'

'I don't belong out there,' she tells the plum tree. 'At school, when I was at school and even last year at university, it was the same. They laugh at me, at the things I say and when they look at me, I can see what they think in their eyes. I'm never going to belong but Karl wants me to and…'

She pulls herself away from the plum tree. Above her the sky has darkened into night and she watches, one by one, the first stars come out. On the night Karl told her he loved her, she'd seen a falling star. She'd never seen one before. 'Look,' she'd whispered. 'Look. It's a portent isn't it, a sign,' and she'd convinced herself she loved him too. Her arms reach out for the plum tree again and that part of her that's still a child trembles and cries out but she won't let herself listen.

Karl loves her. He says she's beautiful and when he looks at her, his dark eyes so frighteningly intense, she has to believe him. It's like a gift, him loving her. It's like he's given her a star to hold, the very star she watched fall that first night…

'But,' she'd whispered. 'But Karl…' She'd wanted to tell him. She had to tell him. 'At school the other girls said… They said I wasn't a proper girl. They liked me, it wasn't that. When things went wrong, they told me because they said I was good at listening but I was…different, they said. I didn't live in a real world and Tiffany Brooks, she was the one they liked best and so did I, Tiffany Brooks said I was fey and then they all laughed and I felt…' She'd bent her head then so her hair could fall over her face, shielding her. 'It's true what they said. I know it is because I feel…'

'Fey?' said Karl and he'd laughed too. 'What sort of word is that?' and then the hot look came into his eyes and he'd kissed her until, breathless, she'd pulled herself away.

'Confidence,' Karl had said later, his mouth going tight. 'All you need, Sinead, is confidence. Your family have been too restrictive. They haven't let you do the things other girls do, go out and have fun. That's going to change now. Once we're married…'

'Married…?'

'Of course. Once you and I are married, everything will be different.'

'But I don't think I want…'

'You love me, don't you? Of course we'll be married. And soon. I don't see any reason for us to wait especially now I've got my degree.'

Her arms around the plum tree, Sinead feels her eyes sting with tears. There's so many things inside her, she can't sort them out. Perhaps that's what's wrong with her. She's always felt too much and, though she's tried, she's never been able to put them into words. But tomorrow it's going to be different. She's getting married. That's what Karl wants and she, she wants it too. Karl's so sure. He's so sure he knows who she is and she…

surely she can be the person he wants. No one else has ever wanted her to be any thing before. No one else has cared.

All at once she hears the back door slam. Someone is calling her. 'Sinead. Sinead.' Her name echoes and re-echoes in the silent garden and she thinks she feels the plum tree shudder.

She looks around her uncertainly. 'I have to go,' she says, pressing her hand against her mouth. 'They're waiting for me and Karl said he might drop in too because…because in the morning…' Her voice falters to a stop but she makes herself go on. 'I don't belong here any more. You know that. I've grown up and when you're grown up, you have to…' All at once she feels calmer. Herself again. Her new self. Sinead Heiland. That's going to be her name. Mrs Karl Heiland. She tightens her lips. 'I'm coming, Mum, I'm coming.' Without looking back, she turns and runs towards the lighted house.

Girl with Fair Hair

It's late winter. After weeks of rain, a few bright days. In the orchard the almonds are in bloom and the first, shy apricots. The peaches are already at pink bud burst and I make my way to the shed to start mixing the bluestone and lime that I'll need for spraying them.

There's a girl at my gate watching me. I stop, frowning. Jeans, dark blue jacket, a tumble of fair hair; all at once she turns and darts away, a mongrel dog at her heels. I stand very still staring after her. The road, such as it is, ends at my place, there's nothing past it except a stand of bedraggled gums and the empty creek bed, a tangle now of blackberries and coarse bracken. They diverted the creek years back when they put in the main highway to Hamilton.

I follow the girl into the road, closing the gate behind me. She's stopped by the trees, her back to me, one hand holding back her hair, the other resting on the dog's head. There's a stillness about her, a waiting, and for some reason I feel my heart stop and then start to beat again very fast.

I go right up to her but before I can say anything the dog runs at me snarling. It's a little brindled bitch with fly-away ears and mad eyes. The girl turns then. I see her face for the first time, wide eyes and tremulous mouth, a child's face, unformed, and she snatches up the dog and holds it against her chest, panting.

'It's all right,' I say, holding out my hands. 'I won't hurt her. Fierce little thing, isn't she?'

The girl's eyes meet mine. They are older than she is. 'She doesn't like men,' she says. 'She's afraid of them. It's because of my stepfather.'

The dog in her arms licks her face and she looks down at it and almost smiles. Then, abruptly, she turns away again. In the silence between us I hear a bird call out, shrill and unexpectedly sweet, and then it's quiet again and there's nothing but the beating of my own heart and the whisper of wind in the forgotten grasses by the fence.

The girl says suddenly, 'Do you think there are animals down there? In the wild bit, I mean. Not here. Here's just the edge.'

'I don't… Rabbits, I suppose. Birds…'

She sets the dog down and pushes back her hair. 'I'd like to live here. A place like this where it's wild. Uncared for. We read about it at school, a hermit in the woods and he made friends with the animals, deer and squirrels and even a bear. I'd like to do that. Live alone…' She turns to me again, her eyes unexpectedly bright. 'Do you do that? Live here all alone like a hermit? Kerrin at school said you did. She said her mother told her. That's why I came. To find out.'

My breath catches in my throat and for a moment I can't answer. So many things, years of things, and she is a child. However old she looks, she has proved herself a child. I close my eyes against the things I won't let myself remember, gun fire, the shouting of soldiers, a girl running, the stripped, grotesque forest.

'I'm not alone,' I say at last. 'I've got my goat, Old Nannie, and Ladycat.' I hesitate. I'm not used to talking. It's not like thinking. Though lately even my thinking's changed. These last few years thinking's become just a series of pictures, good pictures because I know, most of the time, how to make the other ones go away and if they won't, well there's the tablets, the ones the doctor gave me…

The girl's still watching me. She's frowning a bit and it makes her look different, uncertain, so I say quickly, 'I rescued Ladycat. She was caught in a trap. She's all right now, though. Even got herself some kittens. I've put them in a box in the kitchen. They're safe there.'

I shouldn't have said about the trap, though. It's in her eyes. She's seeing that instead of the kittens, Ladycat in the trap, so I say, to distract her, 'Come and see. Come and see Ladycat and her kittens. She's never had a visitor.'

'All right.'

Before I can move away, she reaches out and grabs my hand. I don't want it to mean anything. I swear I don't. But her hand is so small. It rests in mine as if it belongs there, as if…

The girl with the soldiers, her hands, her hands were small too, delicate and I…when it was my turn I had to close my eyes and Smithy, afterwards he made them all laugh at me…

I take a deep breath and we cross the road together and go in my gate. The dog comes with us. It doesn't want to. It's got its tail between its legs and it whines a little but the girl's hand is in mine and though she glances down at it once or twice, she doesn't say anything.

When we reach the back door I stop. 'You'd better leave your dog out here. I'm not sure how Ladycat feels about dogs.'

The girl nods. She kneels by the dog and whispers to it and it settles itself down on the step and I wish I hadn't said anything. It's an ugly little thing. I could have let it come in too.

The kitchen's full of shadows. For a moment I see it as she must. An old room, weary with living. A pile of books on a broken chair, the ash-strewn hearth, the table with the remains of my breakfast, a clutter of dirty dishes and a loaf of bread. The girl makes no comment though she's taken her hand from mine. The loss of it is as real as pain, as real as metal torn from flesh and I shut my eyes again against the screaming voices in the jungle and the acrid smell of smoke.

When I open my eyes, there's only the girl, an image of her against the light, running to the box in the corner. 'Oh. Oh. Can I take them out? Will Ladycat mind? I won't hurt them. Oh, Ladycat, you lucky, lucky girl.'

I sink down in the nearest chair. I'm suddenly very tired. The girl sits cross-legged on the floor, the kittens in her lap and as she bends forward, crooning over them, her hair falls and almost hides her face. It's as though I'm not there, as though I'm a long way off just watching, as though this is one of my pictures. Maybe it is. Maybe it happened a long time ago and I have just remembered or maybe it has yet to happen, a loop of time that will repeat itself over and over again. The girl and the kittens and me, watching. I shudder then. I don't know why. It's her hands I think, her little, delicate hands…

There are too many shadows. They confuse me. And voices. I hear them in the silence. It's like when I wake up after one of the dreams. A girl cries out and some of the soldiers laugh when she tries to run from us… I didn't. I didn't laugh but I…I…

The shadows in the room stretch out toward me, they lie across the floor, the table, they touch for just a moment the girl's soft hair. The girl with the soldiers, she'd got a child's face too, a little half-open mouth and dark eyes. To begin with, she didn't know enough to be frightened…

I stumble to my feet with a little incoherent cry. 'It's time for you to go,' I say roughly. 'It's late. Your mother will be expecting you for your dinner.' I wait for her to answer but it's as if she hasn't heard me.

Outside, by the door, her dog starts to bark, once, twice and then it's quiet again.

My mouth is full of the taste of blood. 'Please,' I whisper to the shadows. 'Please.'

I hear myself start to shout. 'Put the kittens back in the box. It's time for you to go.'

Her eyes go wide. I can't bear the sight of them. I turn away and busy myself with the dishes on the table. 'I don't want your mother to worry,' I whisper. 'It's late. I told you. It's late.'

She doesn't say anything. She gets up obediently and puts the kittens back one by one and then she comes up to me and lays her hand on my arm. 'Thank you,' she says. 'Thank you for showing them to me.'

The steadiness of her eyes reassures me. She's a child, I tell myself, a child, she doesn't know and I make myself walk past the shadows and open the door so her dog can run in.

We walk in silence to the gate. I hesitate, though, before I open it.

'You can come back,' I say. 'Next week if you want. Ladycat and the kittens. They'd…they'd like that.' All at once my throat aches so much I can hardly swallow. 'I never…I never even showed you Old Nannie.'

She doesn't answer. She's got her head down so I can't see her face but I know she won't come back. The shadows, the treacherous shadows, they've broken the connection between us. I close my eyes and by the time I open them again she's almost out of sight. All I can see is the little dog dancing round her feet and the light on her fair hair.

Dilly

I love her. I know I do. Breathless, I tell everyone. Mum. Dad. My sister Kathryn. Michael. I leave him till last because, of course, he's the most important.

He stares at me for a moment and then he goes over to the fireplace and stands there with his back to me. 'Are you sure, Andrea? Are you really sure? After Samantha left us, I never thought anyone…' His stops and fumbles in his pocket for his packet of cigarettes.

'Why wouldn't I love Dilly?' I say. 'She's your child, isn't she? and I love you.'

My voice is wrong, a child's, thin, high, defiant but Michael doesn't notice. He's smoking his cigarette and when he finishes he turns around and his face has changed, has come alive and he's laughing and everything's different. Magic. Somehow I have made magic happen.

A few days later he asks me to marry him.

'Yes, oh, yes.' I see myself suddenly in a swirl of satin and lace, Dilly, solemn-eyed, with a basket of flowers, Kathryn matron of honour in a dark blue cocktail dress…

But… 'Something quiet,' Michael says. 'Samantha insisted on a big wedding, church, music, limousines, the lot but in the end it didn't mean anything, not to her at any rate. I'm not having that this time.'

I twist the engagement ring on my finger. 'Don't…don't you think Dilly would like to be a flower girl?'

'No. She's too shy.'

I bite at my lip and watch the light dance on my ring.

'No,' says Michael again, leaving me and going to the window to stare out into the gathering darkness. 'In any case, Dilly won't be there. Just you and me, Andrea, and the witnesses. Anything else wouldn't be appropriate. You don't need to be a bride. You're going to be Dilly's mother and my wife.'

I lift my head. 'Yes, of course.'

***

In the autumn after we're married, Dilly starts school. Michael makes it a cause for celebration. A special trip to the zoo. A cake with pink icing. Her school things, bag, lunch box, coloured pencils, all wrapped in flowery paper and piled up on the table.

Dilly reaches a tentative hand towards them. 'For me?'

'Of course, silly. Who else is starting school tomorrow?'

Dilly nods. 'I wish…' she whispers but Michael doesn't hear her. He's too busy unwrapping her new backpack.

'Look, it's got your name on it.'

'Yes.'

Afterwards, when Michael's gone into the computer room to watch the news, Dilly pulls at my arm. 'Will it be very bad?'

'Of course not. You'll like it. Other children…there'll be lots of other children for you to make friends with.'

Her eyes meet mine and I stop, disconcerted, because Dilly's not very good with other children and we both know it.

'Read,' I say quickly. 'They'll teach you to read. What about that? Soon you'll be able to read every one of your books.'

'I don't need to. I can make up my own stories from the pictures.'

'That's all very well for now but later…'

She's stopped listening. She reaches across for her box of pencils and tips them out on the table. 'Green, black, purple,' she whispers, her apprehension forgotten.

The secret look's on her face again, the look I don't like, the look that shuts me out. She's like that. Always changing. Shot silk, Kathryn said once, reminding me of a dress our grandmother had when we were little, she changes with the light. I don't think that. I think it's something quite different.

I finish stacking the dishwasher and go back over to her.

'Magenta, black, green.' Her hand hesitates for a moment then darts forward to reposition a pencil. 'Yellow, pink, grey.'

I kneel down and put an arm around her. 'Oh, Dilly,' I whisper. 'It might be bad at first but you'll get used to it. I promise you will.'

She holds herself very still. She's waiting, waiting for me to go back to my work and I say, suddenly desperate, 'I'll miss you. I'll miss you too, Dilly. I'll be all alone when you're at school.'

She looks at me and her mouth tightens and then she looks away again and I feel…I don't know how I feel…ashamed, as if she has caught me spying on her, as if… I get up clumsily and go into the spare room, the room I've planned to make into a nursery though Michael has other ideas…

The next morning when I go in to call Dilly, she's already awake, sitting half dressed on the side of her bed rocking herself backwards and forwards. She looks so small.

'Come on,' I say. 'I'll help you with your uniform and then we'll do your hair. How about plaits? Real schoolgirl plaits?'

She nods and holds up her arms so I can slip her checked uniform over her head.

Her hair's more difficult. It's so fine it slips through my hands like water but in the end I manage. 'There,' I say. 'What do you think? Pretty good, eh?'

Her eyes regard our reflections in the mirror without expression and then she turns her head away.

I finish with her hair, clipping back the loose bits in the front and tying the ends of her plaits with ribbon. 'Come on,' I say. 'Breakfast, and then we'd better be on our way.'

'Are we going through the park by the river?'

'Not this morning. It's quicker the other way.'

She starts to say something but then she stops.

Her hands twist themselves together and I say quickly, 'We can come home that way. This afternoon. Every afternoon if you like because I'll be waiting for you at the gate. You don't have to worry. I'll be there every afternoon waiting for you.'

'Mummy didn't wait,' she whispers. 'We were at the shops and she left me and she didn't come back.'

'I'm your mother now.'

'Yes.' She doesn't mean it, though. The truth's in her eyes.

Without saying anything, I turn and go into the kitchen.

Michael's there by the sink finishing off a last cup of coffee before he leaves for work. 'Where's Dilly? Haven't you got her ready yet?'

At the sound of his voice, she comes running and flings herself into his arms. I don't watch. Tight-lipped, I busy myself with setting out her mug and the chipped bowl with blue flowers that she insists on using for her cereal.

It doesn't take long for us to get to the school. Ten, twelve minutes. I want it to last longer. I don't want to give her up. She already has too many worlds that I can never be part of. But we've reached her classroom. An open door, a crowd of jostling children and her teacher comes forward and takes her hand. So small her hand. It lies in her teacher's…so quiet… I could almost convince myself that she put it there willingly, that her teacher will succeed when all this time I…

'Remember,' I say desperately. 'Remember, Dilly, I'll be waiting for you at the gate, at the gate with the other mothers.'

'Yes.' She lifts her face so I can kiss her and then she's gone, whisked away into a circus world of colour and laughter and bright, tumbling children.

I stand for a moment staring at the closed classroom door and then I turn and walk slowly home.

***

The days take on their own routine. A pattern we fit ourselves into. Mornings, brisk, purposeful, Hawker Street, the lights, the shops, the open school gates, cars, a confusion of children, mothers, shouts, slammed doors, Dilly letting go of my hand and running across the lawn, her face pale and determined, the ribbons of her plaits bright against the grey of her school parka.

The afternoons are different, are our reward. Once we've gone through the park and reached the tangled, untidy river we're ourselves again. The wind in the reeds. Birds. A drift of coloured leaves. Dilly trails behind me, singing to herself, her plaits half undone so her hair spills down her back like foam. I make myself smile then. I'm getting like Dilly. Seeing things that aren't there. Hair is hair.

Winter. I buy Dilly mittens at the market and a pair of rubber boots. 'We'll need them by the river,' I tell her. 'It's muddy now.'

'I'll leave you the car,' Michael says, looking up from his newspaper and frowning. 'You don't want to be walking now the weather's changed. I can get the train into work.'

'Well…' I begin but Dilly interrupts me.

She pulls at her father's arm. 'Please let us walk. We don't even care if it rains. We like it don't we, Mummy?'

'All right, then. Don't you catch cold, either of you.' He's smiling at Dilly, she's laughing in the circle of his arms and it's like I'm not there, like I'm invisible.

I go into the kitchen and start preparing vegetables for a casserole. Mummy, she called me Mummy, I whisper clenching my hands but, I don't care. It's too late. I don't care. I look around me suddenly frightened. It's almost as if I've said it aloud and Michael and Dilly have heard.

Every day the river but every day a different river. Swollen with rain. Angry. Whispering secrets to itself. Spangled with light under an unexpectedly bright sky. Dark and brooding

'Look, Dilly. It's almost spring.' I show her the buds on the willow fronds and in the tangled undergrowth, a spray of white flowers.

Dilly's mouth goes stubborn. 'I guess so. I liked it better before when it was bare.' She picks up a broken stick and throws it into the water. 'The river's a monster,' she says giggling 'A snake monster,' but then her eyes go wide and she whispers, 'The rainbow serpent. We did that at school. The river's the rainbow serpent.'

'Don't be silly.'

She's stopped again. She's found a feather in the grass. 'Look, Andrea, look. The serpent's left me something.' She fumbles with her mittens and bends to pick it up.

For a moment the light's luminous on her hair, her suddenly uplifted face, her hands, Victorian portrait, Little Girl with a Blue Feather.

I bite at my lip and turn away impatiently. 'Come on. It's getting late.'

Behind me, then, something, I'm not sure, a bird perhaps, a caught bird with beating wings…it must be a bird because it's cried out…oh! certainly, certainly a little wild bird…

I turn round. Not a bird. Not a bird at all. Dilly. Dilly falling. Grey parka. A tangle of pale hair. Hands. Her little frantic hands and the dark waiting water.

I stand very still, watching, and then slowly, deliberately, I turn and walk toward the wooden footbridge that leads into Carlyle Street. Beside it there's a clump of flowering grevillea. I bend forward to examine it. Against the stiff foliage the flowers gleam as red as holly berries. A song. A long time ago, a song, Kathryn at the school concert, her voice thin and pure and delicate as spun glass. 'The holly bears a berry as red as any blood and Mary bore sweet Jesus Christ to do poor sinners good...' I take a deep breath and watch my hands smooth down my skirt. 'There won't be any blood,' I whisper fiercely. 'Whatever the river does, there won't be any blood,' and I start to laugh. 'It's taken her, the river, and she must have wanted it because she said...'

Suddenly I'm running, running back along the bank and I'm shouting now, 'Dilly. My little girl. She's fallen in the river. Dilly,' and all the time something else, exultant, is whispering, 'She's gone, she's gone and now Michael will let you have your own child and she, she'll be different, she'll love you and Michael...'

Confusion then. A man with a dog. Two schoolboys. Police. An ambulance. Questions. So many questions and my own voice, so steady, brave even. 'She was right behind me but when I reached the bridge and turned around...the water...she must have fallen in the water...' And underneath everything Kathryn singing and me saying over and over, there won't be any blood, sweet Jesus, sweet Jesus there won't be any blood so it can't have hurt her surely sweet Jesus Christ to do poor sinners good.

The voices in my mind are suddenly quiet. They've found her. They carry her up out of the water and lay her down on the bank. She's so still. A doll. She's like the doll Kathryn had when we were little. I always wanted to play with it but she would never let me...

I stumble forward, 'Dilly. Dilly,' and an ambulance worker comes out from the crowd and covers her gently with a blanket.

Moth

When I get home from the library, my mother tells me Sidonie has been trying to ring me all afternoon. 'I told her you weren't here but she wouldn't listen.'

I let my books slide onto the table and don't answer and Mum adds, her mouth pursed, 'I thought you girls weren't friends any more.'

'Oh, that,' I say softly, letting my fingers trail across my books. 'That doesn't mean anything.'

'Well, aren't you going to ring her back? I told her you would.'

'Yes. Yes, of course.' But I'm smiling to myself and I don't move.

After a while, though, I pick up my books and go to my room. It's quiet there. I need the quietness because once I talk to Sidonie, everything will be changed. It always is. 'Moth,' I whisper. 'I am a moth to her candle flame,' and suddenly I start to shudder so I have to wrap my arms around myself to hold myself still.

It's evening by the time I go into Mum's room to retrieve the cordless telephone. I sit on my bedroom floor, my back against the closed door and wait for Sidonie to answer.

'Where have you been?' Her voice quick, impatient, on the edge of anger. 'You have to get a mobile phone. I've been waiting hours for you to ring back'

I don't answer. I hunch my knees and stare at the circle of light my lamp makes on the pale carpet.

'I have to talk to you. It's important.'

'Yes.'

'Not on the phone. I can't tell you on the phone.'

'Well…'

'You'll have to come here. Mum and Dad have gone out so I can't borrow the car to come and get you but I'll meet you. Remember. We used to do that all the time last year after school. Meet halfway.' She stops and, when she speaks again, I can hardly hear her. 'Please. Please, Michelle. I need you.'

I put my hand up to my throat. I'm shuddering again. Oh, moth, moth…

I'm more than halfway there when she steps out of the shadows to join me. She doesn't say anything and neither do I as I fall into step beside her. Sky, stars, the wavering shadows across the road, a street lamp. She turns her head away. Crescent of cheek, nose and delicate lips. Gazelle-boned, I think; her face is gazelle-boned and, aching, I watch her put her hand up to brush away a strand of falling hair.

When we reach her place, she opens the gate but she has trouble with the front door even though she's left the outside light on. Her hands flutter desperately against the dark wood and I shake my head, confused. I, I am the moth and she, dazzling bright, she is the candle flame…

Once we're in the narrow hallway, though, she's in control again. 'You don't want coffee, do you? I don't want to have to bother with all that.'

'No.'

We both go into her room and sit down, she on her bed and I on the desk chair facing her. Everything's so familiar. Her Renoir print on the wall, her shelf of books, her flounced dressing table. Our own faces, reflected in the mirror, staring at one another. Except….except…all this year, March until September. I have hardly spoken to her…a crowd of girls laughing on the way to lectures…on the lawn in front of the library with a boy whose name I don't know…handing her assignment in late after a maths tutorial… Sidonie…Sidonie, always careful not to look at me, to acknowledge me in case…in case… Outgrown. She has outgrown me. At university, I am still a little schoolgirl, wide-eyed, tangle-haired and she, she…

'Well,' I say at last. 'Well, what is it?'

She laughs then and her eyes slide away from mine and she forces herself to laugh again. 'Can't you guess, Michelle? Really? You can't guess?'

Her mouth twists. It changes her face and makes me turn my head away. When she looks like that, she isn't beautiful and it's her beauty…the aura of her beauty…candle flame, oh candle flame…

'I'm pregnant.'

I feel my mouth go dry. 'Pregnant?'

'You don't have to repeat it. You heard me.'

'I only…'

'You have to help me.' She gets up and goes over to the window. 'I have to get rid of it. As soon as possible. I have to get rid of it and you have to help me.'

Her hands. I stare at her hands against the windowpane. White, white and her profile, pure, a medieval painting and outside, outside the window, the darkness, the unfathomable darkness

'Sidonie, I…I…'

'What else can I do?'

She half turns and I can see now her quivering lips and something happens inside me, the old aching connection and I don't want to feel it but it's there, it's still there and nothing I do will change it.

'Can you imagine it?' she asks. 'Me, with a baby? What would I do with it? A baby. A helpless baby.' Her voice goes hard again. 'I don't like helpless things. You know that.'

'But…but…you can't just kill it.'

'Of course I can. It isn't real anyway. Not yet. It's just cells.'

'No, it…'

'Please. Please, don't. I know what you think and it doesn't help Even if…even if I agreed with you, it wouldn't, it couldn't make any difference. Oh,' she cries and suddenly she's my Sidonie again, Sidonie at high school under the poplar trees, her face earnest and intent, telling me secrets, telling me all the things she daren't tell anyone else. 'I never meant for this to happen. You know I didn't. Games. It was just games. Andrew and Carson and James. They didn't mean anything. They never even knew about one another and even if they had… Games, just games.' She takes a step towards me and it's like the light on her face is burning me. 'A baby's meant to mean something, something important. You believe that, don't you, Michelle, a commitment. It shouldn't be just, just…'

'A child is,' I whisper. 'A child just is. It doesn't have to mean anything. It is itself.'

'Oh, Michelle.' She's turned back to the window and she's drawing shapes on the glass, little quivering shapes that blur and run into one another. 'Whatever. It doesn't matter. I can't have it. You…you do see that, don't you?'

When I don't answer, she shakes her head and starts again. 'I went to the clinic yesterday. That was bad. I can't…I can't go by myself when they…when they…' She takes a deep breath and whirls to face me, her eyes suddenly wide. 'You have to come with me. That's why I rang you. I want you to come with me.'

I don't say anything. I can't.

She runs to me then. She kneels down in front of me and her hands reach out and, before I can stop myself, I take them and hold them safe between my own.

'Please,' she whispers. 'Please. You have to come with me.'

Inside myself, my thoughts gibber and clutch at one another. A baby. A baby in the dark with its big head and transparent, star-fish hands.

With an effort of will, I push her away and hold myself very still. 'I can't, Sidonie. You know I can't. Anything. Anything else but not a baby, not a little unborn baby.'

'But…but…you have to. I can't…I can't go by myself.'

I close my eyes. If I can't see her…her face…her eyes… But it's worse. It's like last year. Truth and beauty Keats said but somehow truth never seemed important to me, only beauty. Her beauty. I could never explain it. My mother, tight-lipped, 'What do you see in her? She uses you. Can't you see that? She just uses you.' It wasn't that. I didn't care about that. It was something else. A shining. The aura of light around her. Always that and the dreadful, dreadful throat-catching beauty…

She reaches up and lays her hand against my cheek. 'You have to come,' she whispers again. 'You love me. You told me. Don't you remember? You told me.'

The art gallery. The floor a lattice of sun-light and shadow and in front of us a portrait of two girls embracing and I said…I said…

I try to turn away. 'But a baby's different.' My voice goes hard, cruel, is her voice. 'You don't need me. Not for this. Not for anything. Anyway what about James, Carson, the other one, what about the baby's father?'

'Stop saying that.' She's angry now 'Stop calling it a baby. It isn't. It isn't.' Her breath catches in her throat. 'I don't love anyone,' she whispers. 'I don't think I can,' and her eyes, wide, dark, look into mine. 'I wanted to love you because you…but I can't. I can't love anyone. It's a game. All of it's a game and now…now…'

A wing of dark hair's fallen across her face so she looks…a child…
oh, Sidonie…a child, a child…

'Sometimes at night I pretend I have the baby and give it to you.
Alison Virginia – see, she even has a name – and I give her to you and you
bring her up for me. You'd do that, wouldn't you, Michelle, take my baby
and pretend it was yours so no one would ever know. You'd protect us,
wouldn't you, my baby and me?.'

I can't speak. I don't have to, though. She knows. She knows me just
as well as I know her.

Her fingers, infinitely tender, trace the curve of my cheek. 'I wish I
could,' she says sadly. 'But you'd love it, wouldn't you? In the end you'd
love it more than me, instead of me. I couldn't bear that.' She gives a
shaky little laugh. 'That's funny, isn't it? Me minding.' She sighs and gets
up. 'She would love you too, she wouldn't be able to help herself and
that would be worse. My baby loving you instead of me.' She sits down
on her bed. 'I want people to love me. Lots of people. It's exciting. I
can make them…' She stops and shakes her head. 'You don't want to
know what I can make them do. And, and all the time I'm, I'm invincible
because I don't love them. It's a game, just a game.' She drops her head
and concentrates on straightening the hem of her skirt. 'It isn't a baby.
You have to believe me. It isn't a baby. It can't be.'

After a while she lifts her head. 'I need you,' she whispers. 'I've never
needed anyone before. You know that. But you…you're different. You
love me. You love me for myself and you'll go on loving me, won't you?
Whatever I do, you'll go on loving me.' All at once she smiles and holds
out her hands to me. 'Please. Say you'll come with me, Michelle. Don't…
don't make me go by myself.'

Her face. The light on it blinds me and I can't help myself. The
dazzling, dazzling light.

'All right.'

I'm crying now but so is she and the light around us splinters into a
thousand diamond stars.

The Lady of Shalott

We always eat our lunch sitting on the wall by the tennis courts, Rachel and Karen and Sally and me. I try to sit next to Sally but it doesn't always work out like that. I swing my legs backwards and forwards and recite poetry to myself.

> 'On either side the river lie
> Long fields of barley and of rye,
> That clothe the wold and meet the sky...'

The words fall into pictures in my mind and I start to smile.

'Stop it, Bryony,' says Sally suddenly. 'Stop banging about with your legs.'

'Yeah,' adds Rachel. 'Why d'you have to do stuff like that, Bryony? 'S like you're still a little kid.'

I turn my head away.

> 'By the margin, willow-veil'd,
> Slide the heavy barges trail'd
> By slow horses...'

It isn't any good. I can't concentrate. Their voices are too loud and I have to listen even though I don't want to.

'Oh, leave her alone,' Karen's saying. 'Who takes any notice of her? So she hasn't got any social graces. Who cares? It's not like she's ever going to meet anyone important.'

I stare at her, open-mouthed. How can she know that? How can anyone know that? And...and...what exactly are social graces? I see the words suddenly in my mind, all embroidered over with little seed pearls like the Lady of Shalott's dress. I sigh and turn my attention back to my sandwich.

But Sally isn't quite ready to give up. 'And, another thing, Bryony. You ought to do something about your hair.'

'My hair?'

'Yes, it looks awful like that. You ought to get it cut. Your face is all right. You're quite pretty really but…' Sally shrugs. 'Karen, don't you think Bryony would look really good if she…'

I hide my clenched hands in my lap. 'I like my hair as it is.'

'But it looks so… Karen, you tell her. Rachel…'

'I'm not going to get my hair cut. Not ever.'

'Oh well, suit yourself. I'm only trying to help.' Sally takes a bite of her apple and looks away. 'People laugh about you, you know. They laugh about you and then they start on about your mother.'

'What's wrong with my mother?'

'Oh, Bryony, don't pretend you don't know. She's weird. Look at the way she wears that old captain's cap. All the little kids think she's a witch.'

I don't say anything. I put the rest of my sandwich in my lunch box and carefully close the lid.

Karen jumps down from the wall. 'Haven't you two finished yet? I put our names down for a softball bat at the sports shed this morning and they'll be closed if you don't hurry up.'

I hesitate. I want to go to the library. I finished my book last night and I won't have time after school because of the bus. I practise saying in my head, 'I'll be with you in a minute, I just…' but the words won't come so in the end I take a deep breath and stumble after them.

***

I like evening best. The sky's all hushed and mysterious then. In the bottlebrush outside my bedroom window the clamour of birds, wattlebirds and New Holland honeyeaters and once, in the summer, a whole lot of musk lorikeets. Their colours glow like jewels. I sit on the floor with my knees hunched up, reading. All sorts of things. My school books. An old medical encyclopedia. A book I found in the shed: *Diary of an Unknown Aviator*. Poetry. Oh, most of all poetry… I push back my hair. 'The pursuit of knowledge,' I say aloud. I like the sound of it. It's as if I'm on a white horse, one of King Arthur's knights on a quest for the Holy Grail. Sir Lancelot, it's like I'm Sir Lancelot…

'On burnish'd hooves his war-horse trode;
From underneath his helmet flow'd
His coal-black curls as on he rode.'

It's got very quiet. My room's full of shadows but I don't mind. I like them. Shadows aren't like people. They don't demand anything of you or ask questions about your mother you can't answer. I lean my cheek against the windowpane. All at once I'm close to tears. The first stars have come out and they blur and dance together. Splinters. They are splinters of light and they… It's not enough. It's never going to be enough. I fling myself down on my bed and put the pillow over my head so my mother won't hear me crying.

***

All at once it's spring, the last week of third term.

'Why do you spend so much time on your homework?' Sally asks. 'The assessment's over. It doesn't count any more.'

I open my mouth. For one minute I think I might be able to tell her but Karen, dumping books on the desk next to us, interrupts.

'She does it to show off. But it only proves how stupid she really is. It won't help her get a job.' She smiles but it's not a proper smile, her eyes are watching me too carefully.

Sally nods. 'It's funny you being so clever at school stuff, Bryony,' she says, frowning. 'You're hopeless at everything else.'

Rachel giggles. 'Like home economics last semester. Remember all the trouble she kept getting into and then, when we did the final exam, she got an A. No one else did. Not even you, Karen.'

'Yeah.' Karen starts scrabbling in her bag for her pencil case. 'That's what I mean. What's the good of it? I bet she still can't cook anything. She can write stuff down but she can't actually do anything.'

Sally's still frowning. 'It's something, though. I mean…'

I start to rearrange my books. I don't want them to see my face. I don't want them to see I mind. They're talking about me like I'm not there, like…like I'm not a real person. I want to be like them, like the other kids I know, all of them laughing, careless, self-assured…not like me…not afraid… I'm afraid all the time and my mother… I don't want to be like my mother but already, already…

'Mad,' screams a voice in my mind. 'Your mother's mad. Every-one knows that and you…you…'

'No,' I whisper. 'No…' but the voice in my mind is laughing and I have to bite down hard on the inside of my mouth to make it stop.

The teacher comes in and starts writing chemistry equations on the blackboard. I open my notebook and let my hair fall forward over my face. That's why I like my hair. It's so long and thick and I'm safe behind it. Very carefully, I start to copy the equations. I like chemistry equations. They're predictable. One side is always balanced by the other. They make sense.

The voice in my mind has gone away. Maybe it won't come back.

***

It's evening again. The bottlebrush outside my window bristles with new flowers. When you touch them, though, they're unexpectedly soft. They're the wrong colour. I don't like the colour red. It's too intrusive. It's the colour of anger.

I've started writing words down in the back of my English exercise book. Aloof. Discreet. Inscrutable. I pretend they're spelling words. But they're not. They're my words, words to describe me, the person I want to be. I want to be an iron hand in a velvet glove. I found that in a book last week. I start to smile. It sounds so strong. Lancelot. It sounds like Sir Lancelot. Distracted, I write very quickly spindrift. I love the word spindrift. When I shut my eyes, I can see it, white spray and the sea all dark and the towering, ominous cliffs. And spangles. I like that too. Spangles of frost on spring grass. I shiver with delight. A poem. It sounds like a poem. But I tighten my lips and cross them out. They are not the right sort of words. They are not dignified enough. They don't command respect. I don't want to be a spindrift and spangles person. I want to be… angry. Anger has power. It can make people do what you want and it isn't afraid. It isn't ever afraid.

I throw my pen down suddenly. It's all coming out wrong. I don't want to be like I am, people laughing at me all the time…but…but…

173

Anger's powerful but it's dangerous too. I know that. It can destroy things. I know that from my mother. It can destroy everything.

***

It's too hot for softball. We fling ourselves down, panting, under the poplar trees at the edge of the oval. Little tender poplar suckers are coming up in the grass. They are so brave. I reach out to touch one. Its leaves shine copper gold in the sun.

Rachel leans back on her elbows. 'Soon as I'm old enough, I'm leaving school. Mum says she can get me a job at the restaurant where she works.'

'I'm not,' says Sally. 'I'm going to do Year Twelve. I want to be a nurse. You have to go to uni for that.'

'I don't care what I do,' says Karen, smoothing down her skirt. 'So long as it pays well, of course. It's afterwards that counts.'

'Afterwards?'

'Well, I'll get married and then we'll…'

I stop listening.

> 'All in the blue unclouded weather
> Thick-jewell'd shone the saddle leather,
> The helmet and the helmet-feather
> Burn'd like one burning flame together,
> As he rode down to Camelot…'

But before I can go on to the next bit, Rachel starts pulling at my arm. 'Come on, Bryony. What about you? What do you want to be?'

'I want to be the Lady of Shalott.'

'But that's just a story. It isn't even true.'

'It is,' I whisper, twisting my hands together in my lap. 'Of course it is. It's just…it's just another kind of truth.' I lift my head. 'I can see it. The island. Sir Lancelot. The leaves falling as she goes down to get the boat and then the mist on the darkening water.'

They're staring at me. Their eyes. I can feel their eyes…wonder…their eyes are wide with wonder and I cry out, 'Oh, don't you understand, she was cursed but, but that didn't matter. None of it could stop her and she wasn't afraid, in the end she wasn't afraid. They couldn't stop her from being who she was.'

Karen makes a sudden impatient exclamation. Her lip curls with contempt. 'You're mad. Sally, Rachel, I've told you before. She's mad. I don't know why you bother with her.'

I wait. Sally…Sally… 'Please,' I whisper. 'Please.'

In the silence I can hear the Lady singing as she unties her boat. Her hair, tangled round her face, is interwoven with tiny flowers. The singing's louder. Birdsong, it's like birdsong after rain. It makes my heart turn over.

All at once I know what it means. Everything. I know what it means. I am the Lady of Shalott. I've always been her. I don't have to be afraid any more. I just have to accept who I am. The things inside me, the things I see that others don't, they're important. They make me who I am and it doesn't matter about anything else just as long as I am true to them. Just as long as I am true to myself.

I take a deep breath. 'It doesn't matter,' I whisper but they've stopped listening; they're talking about something else.

I push back my hair and look around me. Suddenly everything seems bright with sunshine, the grass, the girls, the quivering poplar trees, they take on an added dimension. They shimmer with magic.

'The power of the mind,' I whisper. Then I give a little laugh. I know who I am at last.

I am the Lady of Shalott.